M000074385

Ember's Dragons

ISABEL TILTON

Copyright © 2019 by Isabel Tilton. All rights reserved.

Cover illustration by Janine Hvizdos

This is a work of fiction. Names, characters, businesses, places, events, locales, and incidents are either the products of the author's imagination or used in a fictitious manner. Any resemblance to actual persons, living or dead, or actual events is purely coincidental.

This book or any portion thereof may not be reproduced or used in any manner whatsoever without the express written permission of the publisher except for the use of brief quotations in a scholarly work or book review. For permissions or further information contact Braughler Books LLC at:

info@braughlerbooks.com

Printed in the United States of America
Published by Braughler Books LLC., Springboro, Ohio

First printing, 2020

ISBN: 978-1-970063-42-4 soft cover
ISBN: 978-1-970063-50-9 ebook

Library of Congress Control Number: 2019918099

Ordering information: Special discounts are available on quantity purchases by bookstores, corporations, associations, and others. For details, contact the publisher at:

sales@braughlerbooks.com

or at 937-58-BOOKS

For questions or comments about this book, please write to:

info@braughlerbooks.com

Braughler™
Books
braughlerbooks.com

For Madison

Prologue

A snow-white dragon sat perched on a cliff. Looking below her, she saw her fellow dragons soaring above the canopy, twisting and diving as they pleased. Her eyes shined for a moment as she watched them, forgetting her troubles. Something about the scene calmed her, yet she still felt on edge. She closed her eyes and drew in a breath, trying harder to keep her mind from thinking about her worries.

She opened her eyes and continued to watch the scene unfold, but with a small hint of defeat in her eyes. She knew deep down her anxieties would never cease. It was her job now to face problems that almost seemingly had no solution. She understood that if she didn't, no one else would. The stress she felt was a part of her job, and she was going to have to grin and bear it.

The dragon averted her focus to the setting sun's rays. Dancing across the ocean, it turned the water a deep fiery orange mixed with scarlet. She sighed and glanced behind her, her gentle white scales retracting as the air rushed out of her body. *There is only so much time left. The longer we stay here more of my clan die.* She snorted as she shook her head and roared angrily. *If we leave, we are killed! If we stay, we starve!* The dragon gazed back up to the sky. A brief moment passed while she stood silent. Her body visibly lost tension as the anger she had felt slowly receded back to worry and sadness. *Oh father,* she thought, crestfallen. *You never told me that being Queen would be this hard. You always showed me the good side of things, but never the dark truth that lurked within. We are the last of our kind. My clan is the only one of dragons remaining. If we die, dragons are gone forever.*

Another dragon with deep purple scales walked up next to her. His gait was steady, and his attention focused on the sunset ahead of him. He closed his eyes as he felt the wind on his face. It was laced with salt and land, a deep, earthy scent that was familiar. He allowed his attention to slip and he looked over at the white dragon. A small trickle of smoke escaped his nostrils, signifying he too was under significant stress.

"I know that a difficult time has fallen upon us, but can you promise me no matter what tries to hinder your plan, you will not stop trying?" he asked. His voice was deep, but not gravelly or coarse. He had slightly tilted his head while asking the question, his posture requesting an answer.

"I can try," she sighed. Her head gently tipped to the side as if pondering the request, her eyes not meeting her friend's stern gaze.

"No!" snapped the other dragon with fierce authority. "I won't leave here until you say you will."

"Fine. I will," said the white dragon, clearly annoyed by the purple dragon's antics. He, however, was not quite convinced by her answer and pushed more.

"You know that if you stop trying, that you're breaking

a promise, right?" He leaned closer to the dragon, nudging her shoulder gently with his broad snout.

"Yes…. yes, I know," she snapped, annoyed with his pressuring. But she did not pull away from his touch and allowed him to move away without harm.

"Okay, then," he said. He stepped back and closed his eyes briefly, pausing for a moment before continuing.

"Everything will work out in time," he said, his voice gentler. His tail relaxed and made a sweeping motion across the ground below him, sending dust around the duo's feet. "If you believe that the world will have its way, then it will. Do what you can and worry about what you can control. The rest is beyond us."

The reminder upset her as her mind raced to counter it. "But what if we all die? I can't let that happen. Even if I can't control it, I will still worry."

The dragon turned away from the cliff and hesitated for a moment. *The only thing we have left is hope and the prophecy.* The young leader had to bite back a bitter laugh. *It has resorted to this, us praying that an old hatchling story will resolve our problems.* She flicked her tail before lumbering into the forest. *Although you never truly know,* she thought, *you never truly know.*

1

Ember had to fight back another yawn. She was slouched at a desk, trying to find anything to occupy herself. Although she enjoyed school, this day had not been the most eventful. Only half awake, she listened to teacher after teacher ramble on for hours. When the final bell rang, she released a breath she didn't realize she'd been holding. She quickly gathered her things, shoving them into her worn book bag before finding her friend, Taylor, who normally waited for her.

"Hey!" Taylor chuckled as Ember looked eager to get out, "What's the rush?"

Ember smiled at her friend, happy to hear her laugh. "School was not the most entertaining, needless to say."

"I feel you," said Taylor. Ember saw her face light up as she came up with an idea "Hey, want to hang out later? We can work on chemistry homework together."

With the mention of homework, Ember's face scrunched up. But she answered her friend despite her distaste "Can't," sighed Ember, "You're going to think this is stupid, but ever since those dragon sightings, my parents…"

"Let me guess," groaned Taylor, realizing her friend's

dilemma. "Your parents don't want you out unless it is for school."

"Bingo. That and I also have work."

"That's ridiculous!" complained Taylor, clearly agitated by her friend's parents' rules. "All it is, is a bunch of made up crap to scare people. The news has been making it ten times worse by sounding like it is the end of the world! We all know dragons aren't real."

"Try telling that to my parents," said Ember as she adjusted her bag.

"Well, when all this dies down, maybe then you can come over. Sound like a deal?" Ember knew this was Taylor's way of trying to make light of the situation. She was well aware her parents were not going to let up on the rules anytime soon, but she didn't want to let down her friend.

"Deal," said Ember.

She waved to her friend and headed out the door. The chilly early November air hit her skin, making her shiver. Ember puffed out a jet of air as she looked for her truck. The frenzy of students trying to get out of the parking lot made it hard to spot it. Her attention quickly shifted from trying to pinpoint her truck to the steam coming out of her mouth.

Ember smiled as she drew in another larger breath and exhaled. She watched as a cloud of steam floated in front of her face.

I'm a dragon! She thought smiling. This sudden excitement radiating from Ember on the dreary day turned some heads and earned her a few concerned stares. But she continued to search for her truck.

She found it quickly and hurriedly unlocked it before

hauling herself up into the driver's seat. She blew in her hands to warm up her fingers and wished she'd grabbed gloves that morning. Ember noted she'd need a pair when she went walking that night.

She pressed down on the brake before turning the key and coaxing the older truck to start up. It refused for a moment, but finally roared to life. She cursed at her truck while pulling out of the school parking lot, saying something under her breath about taking it to the junkyard.

Ember pulled out quickly, not wanting to waste any more time at the school. She had things to do. She drove past miles of withered fields. Since the harvest season was over, the fields had returned back to their barren states. Houses that were once hidden by the tall crops were now visible from the road.

Ember pulled into the parking lot of the children's play place where she worked and parked in the back. Part of her longed to break the rules and park closer to the front. She knew then that mad dash to the warm building would be shorter. However, she was not willing to get written up for something that could be very easily avoided. She had just gotten the job and didn't want to lose it for something so trivial. She stayed in the truck for a moment longer, longing to just turn around and go home. She forced herself to get out, knowing full well that work was how she was showing her parents she could hold her own.

Ember did not like children, but she liked working. She always felt she was important and needed at her job, which was something she didn't frequently feel in other areas of her life. She always put all her effort into everything she did, and her outstanding achievement made her a star employee among her co-workers and higher-ups. Some jealous co-workers called her a suck-up, and Ember didn't want others to think this bothered her. But deep down, it did.

She went into work, knowing that dreary days like this led to heavy business. As the traffic ramped up, it became harder for Ember to keep her patience. By her shift's end, she became certain every parent and child were purposely out to start fights with her. She was called out on the prices and the rules, things for which the automatic "corporate makes the rules" reply was almost always given. One person even picked a fight over the color of her uniform.

When she came out, she breathed a heavy sigh of happiness. She wanted nothing more than to take a long walk in the woods, but she had more responsibilities.

When Ember arrived at her home, she pushed open the door and walked inside. She began scurrying around to get the chores she needed to do done.

Her parents had always made her do chores. They weren't hard, and she could usually get them done in a couple of minutes. She would sometimes talk to friends over the phone while she did them, just something to keep her mind occupied. Her parents didn't care when she did them, but expected them done before they came home.

After she was done, she remembered one of the last things she needed to do was her homework. She turned on the TV for background noise, flipped open her chemistry book, and then began to study. It was cut short when the channel turned to breaking news.

Ember saw Taylor's mother, who was a local news reporter, pop up on screen.

"We are live in Maytown, Montana and there is a report

that a creature was seen flying above the city," the reporter said. She was huffing as if she had seen something, and if she didn't say it right then, it would fade from her mind.

Ember rolled her eyes and sighed. The center of Maytown was around 10 miles away. It was a small town and a tight-knit community. If dragons were real, what business would they have in Maytown?

"We have reports of shots fired at the alleged creature; some people say it had characteristics like a dragon. There is a lot of speculation surrounding these events, as they have taken place in many parts of the world." The image on screen shifted, showing a map of the United States with hundreds of red dots.

"The government has stepped up, claiming these are just top-dollar aircraft that look similar to dragons but that was not their intention. They said they are trying to produce a self-flying aircraft with great agility.

"There was another sighting reported in Ridgewood about a hundred miles from Maytown. Officials confirmed in an earlier interview that there was a substance sent to a facility to be tested. Some witnesses claim it looked like blood, however the head of the Ridgewood Board of Chemical Engineering has not responded to our request to speak with him. There is no more information about this situation at this time and we will get it to you as soon as we know.

"There are also reports of a fire downtown. There is no clear evidence if the fire has ties to the dragon sightings. Officials say that it could be possible and are still gathering information at this hour. They are urging people to stay in their homes until they can confirm what is going on."

The reporter took a breath and was clearly happy with herself on the speed of her report. "This is Megan Weaver reporting, back to you, John."

Ember stared dumbfounded at the TV. *This is getting out of hand,* she thought. *My parents aren't going to let me out of the house once they get home. I might as well take a walk out in the woods while I still can.*

She stood up and headed toward a small room near the back of her home where the weapons were stored. For as long as Ember could remember, she had been around and used guns. She began hunting when she turned seven and soon became a skilled hunter, far surpassing her father a few years after that.

Her mother encouraged her to bring one of her father's shotguns out in the woods after a man died on a stretch of land near their town the year before. Since then, she was always more keenly aware of her surroundings while out exploring, but she'd never had any problems. Ember walked into the room, loaded a gun and was about to walk out her back door before she remembered something.

Gloves! She did not want her fingers to get cold enough to make her turn back. She decided to leave her phone at the house. She knew that it was risky, but she did not want her mother calling her in the middle of her hike, telling her to come home.

She stepped outside just as the sun began to set, making the trees cast long shadows across the leaf-covered ground. The air had cooled considerably, and Ember regretted not taking an extra jacket. She decided not to turn back for fear her parents would come back and prevent her from going. She walked along the trails, turning her head to the occasional scramble of wildlife as they tried their best to avoid her.

Ember saw a game trail and decided to veer off her regular path to follow it. As she started down it, she heard a loud crash in the distance. It echoed and caused flocks of birds to fly up around her. She ducked just in time as the creatures flew in a panicked frenzy. She stood up when it was clear and pulled her gun to a readier position and began to walk toward the sound.

The sound was not close; Ember guessed it might have been a mile or two away. She continued through the foliage, the woods providing an earthy scent. For the first time in her life, she was nervous about being in the woods. She stopped once more as she heard the sound again. This time it was closer. She continued to walk toward the sound with caution, her head high and alert and all her muscles tense with anticipation. Soon she saw something through the trees and realized what she had heard were trees falling. She crouched, gripped her gun, and investigated the clearing.

What she saw winded her and caused her hand to fly to her mouth in shock.

"I told you the female would not be here!" bellowed the first dragon, its voice crisp with agitation like newly stripped sheet metal. "Humans live in shelters, not in the open!"

He was black, but the spikes that ran from head to tail, with a large gap from his neck to his wings with no spikes, were a deep gunmetal grey. He also had a few strange red symbols across his body. His eyes were a deep electric blue and blazed with impatience.

"She is here," reassured the second dragon. "She just hasn't arrived yet."

This dragon looked at the other with tense, narrowed green eyes. Its voice sounded much like a female and was incredibly soothing and smooth. The dragon was a deep turquoise with polished silver wings and spikes.

Unlike the other dragon, she did not have any markings and was smaller.

Ember studied the dragons and saw that they stopped when she shifted to get a better view of them. She held her breath trying not to let panic consume her.

Have they heard me?

"Something is near," the black one said. He sniffed the air and approached where Ember was standing.

Ember watched as he stopped and lowered his head, nostrils flaring.

"Come out human, we know you are present." It snarled as its tail lashed lowly. It reminded Ember of a cat about to pounce on its prey.

It might be interesting to watch a cat hunt, but it was a completely different story when you are on the receiving end, Ember thought.

She stayed where she was and pointed the gun at the dragon, her heart racing. When the dragon began to growl and step towards her, she squeezed the trigger. The gun bucked and hit her roughly in the chest, causing her to stumble backwards.

She saw the two dragons jump in surprise and watched the black dragon notice something hit his scales. Ember heard a loud *Clang* and the bullet whizzed past her ear.

"Ignorant human," the dragon laughed cruelly. Ember could hear a growl was creeping its way up the dragon's throat. "Show yourself and I will spare your life."

Ember stepped out of her hiding place while still aiming the gun at the dragon. She knew that this would be the safest option. She was fearful, but determined to survive.

The black dragon bent its head, roughly ripping the gun out of Ember's hands with its strong jaws and tossing it behind him. He stepped back and broke the gun with a loud *crack!* Ember looked up at the dragon with sheer terror. She was now without a weapon to defend herself, and she didn't know if the dragon was going to hold up his end of the deal. Too alarmed to move, she stood cowering below it.

"Y…you're you're a d-d-ra…" she stuttered.

"A dragon?" the beast mused, clearly taking pleasure in the girl's fear. "Well, look here Dalka, the human seems to have knowledge!" The dragon's voice was filled with harsh sarcasm.

He bent his large head and looked Ember in the eyes, snarling. He curled his lip, revealing rows of sharp teeth capable of tearing Ember into pieces. "She may be part of the prophecy, but I bet she may hold over my hunger for at least a moment."

"Enough, Cadell!" said a turquoise dragon coming up from behind the other. "I have let you have your fun long enough. Is this how you are going to treat your partner?" Her voice was far gentler than the dragon threatening her.

The dragon, now known as Cadell, lifted his head from the girl and stepped away looking rather annoyed. The turquoise dragon bent her head near Ember and held her gaze with unwavering green eyes.

"I can see you have met Cadell. My name is Dalka and I am guessing that yours is Ember. We need your help before it is too late."

"You don't need me!" said Ember franticly, backing away from the dragon. "You must have the wrong person!"

"You are Ember Winters, are you not?" asked Dalka, as she walked up to the girl, her emerald eyes studying her tense frame.

"Yes, yes I am Ember Winters." Ember said, carefully backing away as the dragon approached.

"Then you are the human we have been searching for," said Cadell coming up from behind Dalka. He seemed to be much less scornful, but he still remained wary. Ember was unsure whether his aggression was lost due to the other dragon snapping at him or the fact that they seemed to recognize who she was.

"Why do you want me?" asked Ember. She was still scared of the large creatures and unsure if a sudden movement would send them lunging to kill her.

Dalka sighed and lowered herself to the ground. Ember guessed this was the dragon's way of showing the girl she was not going to harm her. By laying down, it would be much harder physically for the dragon to get up and hurt her. Ember, however, eyed the black dragon who still stood behind his friend with a stern, almost annoyed expression.

"When I was still a hatchling, there was always a prophecy that foretold of a young girl helping us. It was spoken that when a disaster comes upon us, a black dragon whose scales were blacker than the dead of night and markings that were a deeper red than an open wound would be born. (This of course turned out to be the 'deer for brains' Cadell.) Soon, the dragon and the girl would save the dragons from sure and utter extinction." The turquoise dragon paused for a moment before bending her large head towards Ember, making the teen take a few steps back. "The girl's name was told to be Ember Winters."

"This is a bad dream," muttered Ember. She didn't want to believe it was happening. "Just a really bad dream."

"I am afraid this is reality," Cadell spat. "So, I would suggest you stop your complaining or I'll—"

"Cadell here was dropped as a hatchling, excuse him," Dalka interrupted as she tossed a menacing glare at the black dragon.

If looks could kill, thought Ember.

A growl rose from Cadell, making Ember shift uneasily. The black dragon lifted his talons and swept his tail, showing his agitation. But he spoke no further.

"So, um, what now?" Ember asked the dragons. She hoped that they knew what she would have to do, but was disappointed when she saw the confused looks on their faces.

"Aren't you supposed to know this? You're the chosen human!" he said, visibly annoyed with the girl's lack of information.

"Oh, but you're the chosen dragon!" snorted Dalka, jeering at her younger partner. "Oh, wise one! Show me your ways! All hail you!"

Her joking face twisted and she became angry in seconds. "Chosen one, my tail! She is not going to have a clue, you fool! She didn't even know we existed until we came barging through her land! And now half the planet knows we're real thanks to *you!*"

Smoke puffed out of Dalka's nostrils making her stress clear, if it had not been made so already. She glared daggers at Cadell, allowing her anger to speak for itself. The tension between the two dragons was becoming almost unbearable as Cadell returned Dalka's glare with almost the same ferocity. Ember suddenly saw a small open wound on Cadell's stomach. "You're hurt…" she trailed off, unsure of how to continue.

"Your foolish race did that to me," growled Cadell. He shifted his weight to reveal the wound further.

The wound was clearly a bullet wound, the flesh an open hole that seeped blood every time the dragon breathed. Ember inwardly cringed, thinking about the pain and discomfort the dragon must be in.

"Is that why there was talk of blood on the news?" asked Ember. She almost regretted asking when the dragons became concerned. Both of their heads perked like birds who heard danger approaching.

"Blood?" asked Dalka, coming closer. "Where?"

"Somewhere in the city. I don't know! I just saw it in the news. I knew some people took it for testing, but the—"

"*Testing?*" snarled Dalka "You really messed up this time, Cadell! I told you to fly high and not have your stomach exposed."

"Well, I…" The snarky dragon's demeanor was suddenly extinguished by the other dragon's anger towards him.

"Cadell," snapped Dalka. Ember could see she wasn't in the mood for excuses. Her tail thrashed greatly, showing her impatience.

"Look, Dalka, is it?" asked Ember pulling the dragon's attention away from the other. The turquoise dragon looked back at her and nodded in confirmation. Ember continued, "You can't stay here. You'll be killed."

"With your permission, we would like to stay on your

land," said Dalka, her eyes pleading.

Ember fought with herself internally for a moment, pondering the dragons request. She could not find anything good in letting them stay, but she didn't want to say no. She looked down at her feet, shifting her weight as she formulated her response.

"I, I don't know. I'm incredibly overwhelmed. How do I know you're not going to kill me or my family?" asked Ember, narrowing her gaze.

"If we wanted to hurt you, we would have already," pointed out Dalka. "Besides, we only eat big game like deer."

"Just for tonight." Ember sighed as she gave in. "My parents will be home soon. I must go."

She began to jog away before she heard Dalka call her name.

"Sorry about your stick," she said glancing over at the gun which lay broken in the center of the clearing. Cadell had his back turned to the girl and had not seen her leave.

Ember was confused for a moment until she caught on.

"My gun? Oh, it's okay. Sorry I tried to shoot you," said Ember. "I'll see what I can do to stay home tomorrow from school so we can sort this out."

With that, she ran, pushing her legs faster and faster, blood rushing through her ears. The fear caught up with her, fueling her legs to go faster. Her mind raced with ways she could excuse what she had done, but she could find none. She slowed to a jog as she neared her home and calmed her breathing as she walked up the stairs of her deck.

She hesitated a bit at the door. She did not want to confront her father. Her mom was a very sweet and kind woman. She was the one who made her carry a gun and the one who didn't want her to go out because of the news, but her father…was different.

He used to be a good father, but after he lost his job as a salesman, he was forced to get a job in retail. He took to drinking to hide his shame.

She shook her head. This was her *father*; he was supposed to take care of her and help her, right? He would only care that she was safe, and not about the fact she lost (actually had a dragon step on) his gun. Ember stood at the door a bit longer, biting her nail and taking a breath before she mustered up the courage to go in.

She entered through the back door. She smelled dinner cooking in the kitchen. When she walked in, Ember saw her mom flipping pancakes and her father with a bottle of beer in his hand. His head was down on the table and he looked like he was passed out. He looked up to see Ember come in.

"Where is me gun?" He slurred. Ember watched as he blinked, guessing it was an attempt to see through his blurred vision.

"Um, I saw a mountain lion and it chased me and I dropped it." Ember scrambled to come up with an excuse. She surprised herself when the lie came out quickly.

"You dropped meh gun." her father said calmly. Ember knew beneath the calm was a deadly anger about to explode.

"Yes?" she said slowly, waiting for the backlash.

"*YOU IDIOTIC GIRL!*" he yelled, standing up his fist smacking the table. He stood shakily, breathing heavily. The empty glasses on the table wobbled dangerously, threatening to fall over.

There it is, she thought, moving backwards away from him.

Ember saw her mother move over to her father and put her hands gently on his chest. Just like beauty and the beast, her mother was the only person who could calm her angry father. He wouldn't dare do anything to hurt Ember's mother, but when it came to his own flesh and blood, there were blurred lines.

"Honey, it was an accident," her mother soothed her husband gently as if trying to calm a snarling dog. "Ember, I want you to go out there tomorrow and search for that gun, okay?"

Ember nodded as her father sat down heavily in the chair. He stared at her angrily and took a swig of beer before placing his head between his hands. Ember's mother came up to her and whispered in her ear.

"He has a couple spare guns in the gun room," she said as she squeezed her daughter's shoulder. It was her way of saying that everything was going to be okay. "Grab one before you leave."

Her mom served dinner and it remained quiet throughout. It was something Ember was grateful for. It gave her time to think and shift through her thoughts. Standing, she excused herself and headed up to her room. She knew she would have to think of a way to act sick so she could stay with the dragons the next day. With an inward sigh, Ember decided she would work on that later.

She put her attention on her homework to take her mind off of what had transpired. When she could not focus anymore, she leaned back and looked out her window. The sunset was just about over, making the sky a dark blue and black.

Collapsing on her bed, she stared up at the ceiling. Thoughts and unanswered questions whirled around in her mind. She felt a deep void within her chest. It felt like a black hole that sucked everything good in her life away. It was exhausting and it made her feel vulnerable and useless.

Ember wasn't entirely sure what caused the pain. She felt it was the relationships she struggled to keep together at home and school. She also felt it was the unexpected visitors she was secretly housing in her woods.

Whatever was bringing her down, it was draining her of the vigor she once had. It made her afraid.

She closed her eyes and breathed deeply, imagining the air rushing in was cooling her insides.

I can't be the chosen one, Ember thought. *I'm just a normal girl!* But deep down Ember knew that wasn't true.

2

The next morning, Ember succeeded in acting sick. She was happy that her plan worked, as she was fearful her parents would see through her act. She took another gun from the gun room, loaded it and gathered an emergency kit. She figured that maybe helping the large creatures would prevent them from attacking her, but she also pitied the dragons. With supplies in hand, she set out with wavering confidence. Her stomach did flips on the way to them and she wondered if they had bothered to stay. She silently wished that they had moved on.

Maybe I went crazy or something. But she then wondered what was scarier. Losing sanity or having the creatures be real. She noted that Dalka *had* said she did not want to hurt her. Ember wasn't worried about Dalka. Even though she was a bit snarky, it was because she had to put up with the black dragon. Ember gave her credit that she didn't snap even more.

The black dragon, Cadell, was a different story. Ember noticed he was rash and violent. She wondered if his demeanor was really how he was deep down. She saw him submit to Dalka, so she at least saw he had some morals.

But she still reminded herself they were both incredibly dangerous beings, capable of killing her before she even had time to register what was going on. It was a daunting thought, but she pressed forward. She felt like she was doing something right by returning to them.

When she entered the clearing, she saw they were still there. Cadell was sitting under the shade of a large oak tree, while Dalka laid in the rays of the morning sun. Dalka looked at the approaching human with a puzzled expression, cocking her head.

Ember took a step back at the dragon's puzzled expression, fearing she had done something wrong by returning.

"Why do you still bring your weapon stick?" she asked, eyeing the weapon. We've already established we won't hurt you."

They think that I would take their word for it. She gently squeezed the handle of the gun as a reminder of its presence. She was aware it was useless against the beast, but she brought it as more as a comfort.

"It is dangerous out in these woods," she said.

"More dangerous than us?" growled Cadell, lifting his head from underneath the shade of the oak. "I think not."

Dalka shot a glare at Cadell and turned again to face Ember. As if sensing her uneasiness around the snarky dragon, Dalka offered Ember a small smile.

"Do not fear him," Dalka told her gently. "He is a wounded soul. He will not harm anyone. Well, at least not you."

It didn't make Ember feel much better and she continued to eye the black dragon.

"I can guess you have a lot of questions," said Dalka."

"I'm guessing you do as well." Ember said looking up at the dragon with a small grin.

"More than you know," Dalka sighed.

Dalka settled down on the ground and Ember sat a respectful distance away, leaning against a tree. She left her gun and the emergency kit near the entrance of the clearing where Cadell was.

"How come we did not know you were real?" Ember started.

"That is a good question. I honestly wonder how we really managed to disappear from existence as well. We can see that your kind knows *of* us, but didn't really know we were alive or real. Humans depicted us as evil, cruel creatures, capable of breathing fire and demolishing cities in one breath. Am I wrong?" Dalka asked, peering at the girl.

"No, no you're not wrong." Ember replied.

The dragon closed her eyes in a brief nod before opening them and continuing. "We used to live in harmony with humans centuries ago, back when I was not as old and Cadell was still quite young. It was when a group of rebel dragons attacked the humans in cold blood that humans began to fear us. We were forced to retreat to an island, as our kind began to be hunted and killed by your advancing technology. Organizations were created to find and kill us all. We retreated to live on a huge island. It's in the Atlantic Ocean, around a place you humans call a triangle…"

"The Bermuda Triangle?" Ember asked.

"Yes. That's it. It always confused me, though; it looks nothing like a triangle," said Dalka. "We have gone to great lengths to protect our island, even shooting down your planes and ships that passed by. We cannot risk being discovered. We do not like killing humans, and most dragons do not dislike your race. But after your kind began to destroy us, many have turned sour. We, however, do not act out in rash impulses like your species. Shooting down your kind is not a desire or a thirst for human blood, but rather a need to protect ourselves. We don't want to...but we must."

"So, you are what are making our planes disappear!!" Ember gasped. It all made sense now; that was why it was a mystery. She knew if someone knew it was the dragons, it was easily lost in the millions of conspiracy theories.

She was unsure how to process it. She wasn't angry with them; they were only trying to protect themselves. But then again, she thought of all the innocent people who died. She felt more anger at the rebel dragons for killing people and starting the conflict between humans and dragons. Ember strongly believed from what she had heard thus far that they were to blame.

"We are sorry we have caused your race much grief." said Dalka sadly. "There was no other way. But I will tell you the main reason we are here. A disease struck our food source and we have tried everything. It has killed thousands of our prey and our dragons. If we ingest the infected prey, we die too. The prophecy told of you, our last hope. Since we have disappeared and few of your race know of our existence, I fear we have caused much disturbance. Your kind has already killed a few dragons who have tried to reach you. Cadell and I were very lucky to have gotten this far."

"I am very sorry my race has hurt you as well," Ember told Dalka, as she realized how both races were to blame for the clash between them. "What does the prophecy say I do? Or if it is even me. There are other Ember Winters out there," she pointed out with hope that the two dragons would rethink their decision to come to her.

"Cadell sensed you," Dalka replied gently. "That is how we found you."

Ember took a deep breath to steady herself. It was a lot to take in. Although, she thought she was handling it quite well.

"As for what you can do, I am unsure of that." Dalka continued. "We were hoping you would know, but I found that to be wrong the moment you stumbled upon us."

"So, do we just sit and wait?" snapped Cadell. He had obviously been listening silently and Ember jumped at his sudden intrusion. "I can't stand doing nothing."

"I'm afraid so," Dalka sighed.

Ember stood and watched the brief interaction between the two dragons when a question suddenly hit her.

"How can you talk to me?" Ember asked.

"Well…all dragons are required to learn all languages," Dalka explained, "just in case we did need to have contact with humans. This has been one of the smartest choices that our queen has ever made. However, back in the years when we were allied with humans, the majority spoke English so our race adapted an English tongue to be our natural and first language."

"Queen?" Ember said as she heard the royalty term.

"There is a lot to our social structure, and I would be here for a long time if I tried to explain it all." Dalka told the girl. "Each clan of dragons has a king and queen," Dalka said, "Our queen doesn't have a mate, so our clan doesn't have a king."

"Are there other clans?" asked Ember. She was excited

now that she understood some of what was happening. "Do you have different species of dragons? How many more—"

A growl rose from Cadell cutting Ember off as smoke puffed out of his nostrils. He turned his head and looked at the two in the clearing.

"That's always the first thing humans seem to question!" He roared. "Why can't humans have some sort of decency and just keep their tiny useless noses in their own business?"

"Cadell, enough!" snapped Dalka. "I'm sorry Ember. It's a sensitive subject between us."

Dalka looked down a moment, closing her eyes.

"I understand if you don't wish to talk about it," Ember said to Dalka.

"No, it's alright," she replied returning her gaze to Ember. "We are the last clan of dragons remaining. The island is very large and held many clans. But when the disease struck, our race began to get sick and die. Soon, there was only one clan left, us."

Dalka went silent for a moment and looked away once more. The look on the turquoise dragon's face was enough to break Ember's heart. She decided she didn't want to cause the dragons to reflect on their troubles anymore and to steer away from the topic. She nodded in understanding and stood. She walked over to the emergency kit and picked it up.

"I brought this," she said, shifting the large kit so Cadell could see it. The black dragon had lifted his head to look at her when she began to move. "I took some medical classes, I don't know how much it will do, but I thought it might help you, Cadell."

"I don't need your help, Human," snapped Cadell, scrunching up his face.

"Cadell," warned Dalka. "Let her help you. I am not going to have you injured much longer. I don't know how much more of your complaining I can bear."

With an angry growl, Cadell laid down on his side exposing his sensitive underside. Ember saw that a bullet would not kill a dragon, but it would be enough to cause it to bleed and induce pain.

She approached the dragon uneasily. She was expecting him to whirl around and try and attack her at any moment. She could see the dragon viably sigh when she hesitated.

"I'm not going to tear your head off right now," Cadell said. His voice was still snarky but had lost its earlier venom. "Just get the damn thing out."

Ember touched gently under the wound first and was surprised. The underside of Cadell felt smooth, it reminded her much of a snake. She felt around the wound until she found the lump of the bullet. Taking the tweezers, she was able to get the bullet out. The wound began to bleed heavily and she stuffed it with gauze. She then cleaned out the wound and bandaged it up as well as she could. She reached up to pat Cadell on the shoulder and thought better of it.

"You're too valuable to harm. Go ahead and feel my scales if you're curious." he said flipping back on his feet.

Ember reached up slowly and touched his scales. They were hard, but flexible. They were smooth and shiny, reflecting the light of the morning sun.

"Wow!" Ember gasped.

"You humans," said Cadell, "are amused by the smallest of things."

He began to stand and Ember backed away. She turned

to look at Dalka, but soon looked back at Cadell when she heard a loud crack.

Cadell lifted his large foot, and Ember saw what was left of her gun.

"Oops!" was all Cadell said before Dalka's tail collided with Cadell's head.

"Cadell, you idiot!" Dalka snapped.

Ember just stood with her hands on her hips trying to hide a laugh, but she could not stop the smile that came upon her face. But soon that smile faded and she began to panic.

"How do I cover this one up?"

. . . . .

Ember's curiosity about the dragons had gotten the best of her. After she met the dragons, all she wanted to do was learn more about them. She constantly was watching movies about dragons, reading about them, and any spare time she had was spent with the dragons and not with her friends.

One thing that spiked her interest was the Bermuda Triangle incidents.

Two aircrafts disappeared on the same day in 1945, and a total of three that year.

In 1948, 25 people on a passenger plane were lost.

Some boats disappeared as far back as the 1400s.

Ember was shocked as the list of the dead scrolled past her computer screen. There were so many lives lost. It made her sad, and even sometimes angry at the dragons. But she could not find it in her to speak about it to them.

She began to be more distant from those around her. Ember's mind became distracted as she juggled what to do with the two creatures she harbored. Although she heeded the dragons' warning of not telling others about them, she did it more out of her own selfishness. She didn't want others to know about them; she wanted the experience to herself.

Her friends did not let her odd behavior go unnoticed. After a few weeks of this change, Taylor and a few other girls had approached Ember.

"Hey girl!" Taylor said walking up to Ember, whose nose was stuck in a new book she had found in the library. Taylor was clearly hiding her agitation, but Ember guessed she controlled it in hopes of getting to the bottom of her change.

"Hi," she mumbled, not paying much attention to the girls who had come up to her.

"Alright, that's enough," said Taylor, snatching the book from her and looking down at the page Ember was reading.

"Hmm, dragons?" Taylor asked mockingly. "So, what's with the sudden new interest in dragons all of the sudden? Trying to figure out how to kill them so you can get back to us? I bet that would convince your parents they are all gone."

That struck a nerve and Ember's face scrunched up in anger.

"What? No!" Ember snapped, reaching for the book. "Hey! Give It back!"

"Not until you tell me what has been going on," Taylor simply stated. "Do you have a new boy toy?"

Ember glared and stood to face her friend. "If it was any of your concern, I would tell you!" she snapped. It really was none of their concern, the dragons were *her* secret. She didn't want to share them with anyone else. Ember knew deep down that it was selfish, but she did not mind.

Taylor huffed angrily and matched Ember's temper with her own. "What's your problem, Ember?"

"Nothing!" Ember huffed. She could feel her anger rising.

"Really?" said Taylor, feeling pressured by her friend.

Ember paused, unsure how to answer that question.

"Well, you're always in my face all the time!" she yelled.

"No, I am trying to figure out what's wrong," Taylor replied more gently. Ember saw Taylor had lowered her voice when she realized the situation was escalating more than she liked. "You're my best friend Ember; when something is wrong, I want to know so I can help you."

"I don't have a problem," Ember snapped. "And I don't want your help."

"But something is clearly wrong, you never just ignore me, and you haven't answered my texts or calls. Something's up."

"Fine, *you're* my problem, now leave me alone!"

Taylor looked at Ember for a moment, and Ember could have sworn sadness crossed Taylor's face for a brief moment before she handed the book back to Ember angrily. "Here's your stupid book," she snapped, turning around and walking away. "I hope you're happy now."

Ember watched her go, guilt deep in her chest, but she didn't notice it because of the anger boiling within her.

She reflected on the argument on her drive home, the longer she thought about it, the more guilty she felt. Ember pushed it aside as she walked through the door of her home. She decided she wouldn't grab another gun. She did not want to risk Cadell breaking another. She had almost gotten in real trouble for the first one, seeing that she wasn't even supposed to be out of the house. Luckily, neither her father nor her mother had noticed the disappearance of the second one. When or if they did, she would be in even more trouble. Her mother still was not letting her out of the house except for school, and her father just loved his guns. No one touched his guns.

She closed her eyes in a silent prayer that she would be able to get away with it before pushing open the doors and setting out.

She took the quickest route she knew to the dragons, before walking into the clearing.

"Cadell! Dalka! I'm ba—" Her words stopped. She looked around to see the dragons were not there.

Panic gripped her stomach as she walked around the clearing. *They were here every other time I came here,* she thought frantically. *What difference is there now?* She almost began to cry as she searched for them.

Although Ember had only known them less than a week, she could feel herself already getting attached to the two dragons. She had to remind herself that unlike the other animals she had learned about and been around, the dragons were capable on their own. They were self-aware, able to communicate, and Ember could even argue that their intelligence rivaled that of humans. She sat down in the middle of the clearing with her head between her hands and knees. *I should have known that they were going to leave me. I knew it was too good to be true. They must have found the other Ember Winters.* She clutched a handful of dirt in her fist as the tears she had been holding back fell down her cheeks.

"I left my best friend for them," she said to herself sniffing.

Yet, deep within, Ember felt a pull telling her it was not true. She knew that losing her friends was nothing but her own doing, but pushing it away seemed to be the best way of coping with the reality.

"You didn't leave anyone for us," a gentle voice said behind her.

Ember jumped and whirled around to face Dalka, letting the dirt she had clutched drop to the ground.

"I need you to promise me that your relationship with us will not hinder your relationships with others," the dragon said sternly. The words were firm, but warm.

"I promise." Ember sniffed before standing and approaching the dragon. She couldn't help but obey the dragon's wishes. She was happy they had returned and wanted them to stay.

She looked behind Dalka and saw Cadell coming. Dalka moved to the side to let him through and he approached Ember. He bent his head and touched her cheek, pulling back with a snort.

"Dalka! The human is leaking!" he said in shock mixed with disgusted confusion.

Then Dalka looked down at Ember with concern and back at Cadell. Her reaction was much tamer as she surveyed the scene with a level-headed gaze. Ember watched as the gears in the dragon's mind turned. When Dalka looked like she decided she could not come up with an answer, she asked the source of the problem.

"You're right!" she said, bending down to Ember. "Are you okay, small one?"

"Yeah," Ember said, laughing and wiping the tears away. "It's called crying, humans do it when they are sad, angry, or really, really happy."

"Which one of those are you feeling?" asked Dalka concern for her new friend in her gaze.

"I was sad," said Ember, tucking a stray piece of hair behind her ear in embarrassment as she looked down.

"Why were you sad?" piped in Cadell. He had lost his disgusted face and was now concerned. All former emotions, both foul and angry, had long disappeared. It was now hidden by his concern.

"Because I thought that you left me," said Ember. She didn't want to admit it, but being stared down by the two large creatures gave her no out.

Dalka walked up to Ember and pressed her warm nose to Ember's cheek.

"Don't worry, Ember," she said softly as she gently pulled away from her reassuring gesture. "We aren't going anywhere."

"Good. I really like having you guys around," she laughed. "It is odd, I really feel a pull to you both."

"Must be the prophecy's doing," Cadell snorted. "It has a knack for that."

Dalka withdrew her head back and Ember saw her attention focused on something behind her. She turned around to see an oddly shaped jewel on the ground where she had sat moments before.

She walked over to it and picked it up. It was a lightly colored pink, and Ember could see it looked like someone had squeezed the jewel with their fist. When she curled her hand around the jewel, she saw that the imprints matched her hand perfectly.

It took her a moment to realize that it was next to the small hole she had made when she grabbed a handful of dirt.

Baffled, she brought the jewel back to Dalka for her to inspect. Both dragons stared down at the jewel in confusion and curiosity. Ember brought it to Dalka who sniffed it cautiously and nudged it with her nose. She drew back, gasping.

"That's impossible!" Dalka gasped.

"What?" Ember said dropping the odd jewel on the ground before jumping back. "Is it going to explode?"

"Don't drop it!" snapped Dalka with frantic anxiety "That's Merocomee!"

"Mero-what?" asked Ember quickly retrieving the jewel from the ground in an effort to calm the exasperated dragon.

"Merocomee!" Dalka repeated. "It's not a diamond, rock, or stone! It's medicine!"

Dalka shook her large head and looked back at Cadell with a mixture of happiness and awe.

"I knew the prophecy foretold that you held powers, but I didn't even fathom they would be this useful!" Dalka's voice was a pitch higher. Dalka couldn't hide her excitement as she swept her tail quickly back and forth.

When Ember looked at Cadell, she saw that he even had a small smile on his face. Ember was taken aback by the dragon's sudden show of good emotion.

"What is Merocomee?" questioned Ember.

"Merocomee is a medicine that can cure almost any illness," Dalka said, "Although it is a very powerful medicine, it is incredibly rare."

"Where does it come from?" asked Ember.

"No one really knows," said Dalka. "That is why we are friends with some humans, as they have managed to find it somehow. We have only come across it a mere handful of times. I have encountered it once in my life, and its smell is one that I will never forget."

Ember lifted the Merocomee up and breathed in. A lovely scent filled her nostrils. Similar to a flower, but sweeter like honey. It reminded her a lot of a new spring day, filled with life.

"It smells beautiful," Ember gasped inspecting the jewel in her hands.

"Indeed," said Dalka.

"Try and do it again," Cadell said coming up to her.

"Ok!" said Ember, returning to the spot she had grabbed the dirt.

She took a handful and squeezed it with all her might, closing her eyes. When she opened her hand, the dirt was still there. Aggravated, she tried once more. When she opened her hand to reveal the dirt still in its earthy state, she huffed in frustration.

"I don't understand!" she yelled, throwing the dirt back on the ground. "It worked before!"

"Try again!" snarled Cadell.

Before Ember had a chance to do anything else, Dalka interrupted.

"It's okay, Ember," she soothed. "At least we know you have the ability to do it. Your power must have been released when you were under a lot of stress."

Ember nodded still fuming. She turned her head up to Dalka, blinking slowly.

"Why weren't you here when I got back?" Ember asked.

"That is a story for another day," Dalka said laughing. The dragon almost seemed embarrassed. "Once everything settles down, we can discuss that matter."

Ember turned her gaze downcast, disappointed, but did not say anything. Dalka chuckled and lowered her head down to the girl.

"All in time, Ember," she said. "All in time."

3

It had been about a month since Ember met the dragons, but to her it seemed only a mere handful of days. It became difficult to manage her social life, as well as handling the dragons, losing her friends only proved the point further. She went to school and work, paying visits to the dragons every day before her parents came home. Her knowledge of the creatures grew as she communicated with them and did research in her own time. She found that they had two weak spots, one was their stomach and the other was between their shoulder blades where the spikes were absent. She taught the dragons about humans, although they knew some, she still needed to teach them that a gun wasn't a stick and her phone was not food. (Much to Ember's horror, Cadell nearly ate it.)

Ember noticed that they were uncultured. Their speech and hesitant tongue showed that although they were educated in English, they had adopted it from another age. They spoke with the intelligence of ancients, and had done their best to lower themselves to Ember's level and learn the human speech patterns of the modern world.

All the events prior led to Ember about to get on Cadell's back in the clearing. She tried her best to swallow her nervousness as she settled herself.

"Are you sure you're okay with this?" asked Ember uneasily as she peered at the dragon's head. Although she was unable to meet his gaze, she glanced up at him anyway.

"Well, if we are partners, then I might as well get used to the circumstances," replied Cadell. His voice seemed bored as if he had better things to do.

"Well, okay then," said Ember as the dragon shifted impatiently beside her.

Cadell lowered himself to the ground so Ember could climb on. Although Cadell was ready, Ember was not and she hesitated.

"I'm not getting any younger," Cadell rumbled from beside her. His electric blue eyes locked with her anxiety-ridden hazel ones. The two of them, even though different, were able to hold a moment of mutual awareness and understand one another's position.

"I am just not...keen on the idea of getting on you," Ember mumbled, breaking the gaze first. She looked at the ground, kicking a loose pebble.

The black dragon remained quiet as if considering what the girl had said. When Cadell did not reply after a moment of silence, Ember looked back up at him. It was when they locked eyes again that the dragon seemed to get an idea. He grinned and Ember grew uneasy.

"Well then, I'll just put you on me," Cadell said as he shifted quickly.

He bent his large head and snatched the back of her shirt and lifted the girl up.

"Hey!" shouted Ember. "Hey! What are you doing?" She struggled to get away, startled by the sudden movement.

Cadell said nothing, and Ember heard him snuffing out a growl. She figured he was debating on tossing her. Despite his obvious disdain, he turned around and put Ember on his shoulder blades. Grabbing onto one of Cadell's nearest spikes, Ember settled herself as her heart pounded loudly in her chest, panic slowly fading. Soon Cadell began to rise and Ember let out an alarmed gasp before closing her eyes. When Cadell stopped, she opened them.

What she saw took her breath away.

She saw trees as far as the eye could see and mountains that formed off in the distance. The sun was just beginning to set, casting a red glow on Ember and the dragons. The scene distracted her from her fear. She drank in the sights and her mind began to wonder as she watched a hawk fly from a nearby oak.

"Wow," she gasped, "It's beautiful."

Turning her head as the large bird flew, Cadell followed Ember's gaze as she watched the hawk fade off. He exhaled, bringing Ember out of her thoughts.

"This," Cadell said, "This I can agree on, kid."

Ember felt Cadell's muscles flex underneath her and she gripped tighter with her thighs.

"What are you doing?" She asked hesitantly.

"Walking," stated Cadell matter-of-factly. "Am I not allowed to perform a forward motion?"

Ember chose not to reply, and rather focused her attention on her seating, trying to remain balanced which proved not to be hard. Cadell's broad shoulders made for a perfect seat. As much as she didn't want to admit it, she found her earlier fears unnecessary. She felt quite safe upon the back of the dragon.

Cadell began walking at a slower pace around the clearing. He walked a few circles before turning and going the
opposite direction. He went faster, but Ember had finally
grown more comfortable and took the change in pace in
stride.

"You didn't sound alarmed this time," Cadell said
smugly.

Ember huffed as she fought to defend her pride. "Oh,
shut up."

Cadell stopped and looked over at Dalka. His head
cocked, like a confused puppy. Ember was suddenly lurched
forward by a sudden stop and peered down to see what the
issue was.

"What was that for?" she snapped.

"I feel so much stronger!" he said to Dalka with no
intention to answer Ember.

Cadell let out a loud roar, shaking Ember to the core
as she struggled to cover her ears. She saw red out of the
corner of her eyes and looked down. Bewildered, she saw
that Cadell's markings were beginning to glow a brighter
red. She gasped and looked up at Dalka, who also looked
at Cadell with awe.

"Your powers are strange indeed," said Dalka, walking
up to Cadell and nudging his markings. "They radiate nothing but light! I have never heard of an occurrence like this
happening before."

Dalka's nonplused expression worried Ember and she
peered at the smaller turquoise dragon. "I take it that this
is not normal?"

"No," replied Dalka looking up at Ember. "I cannot
seem to scientifically come up with an answer of why this

is happening, but I have a strong suspicion that it has something to do with you."

Dalka turned and walked around Cadell, who stood still seeming to enjoy the power that radiated from him.

"Although," Dalka began again. "It begs the question of how far the powers extend. I do not feel anything, but if she came upon my back would she have the same effect?"

Cadell only grunted at the questions, not caring much about the older dragon's musing. He lowered himself so Ember could get off. When Ember swung her legs over, she shook her head.

"I don't understand any of this!" she said. "How come I had none of these abilities, or powers, or whatever they are, before?"

"I believe you had these gifts before, Ember," replied Dalka. "It's just that you didn't know you had them and didn't know how to harness them. And, as from what we have witnessed thus far, they are most prevalent when we are around." Dalka's look grew softer, "And Ember, these abilities are a gift," she said gently.

Nodding, she turned back to Cadell and offered a small smile. "Thank you for the ride," she said.

"Sure," Cadell said lamely. "Next time, we will go on a real ride. We will go flying."

"Have you lost your mind?" Ember said, glaring coldly at Cadell. "If you think I'll fly with you, you're insane."

Cadell cocked his head in curiosity. A look so innocent that it made Ember want to laugh. "I can assure you that my mind is right here. And I am unsure what insane is."

"It's not a thing," Ember began, "it's like going crazy in the mind."

"What's a crazy?" Cadell questioned.

"It's a...well...when your mental health is not very good."

"But I have excellent mental health," Cadell reasoned, becoming agitated by Ember's accusation. "Unless you think otherwise."

"It's just an expression," Ember explained quickly seeing the dragon's growing anger.

He dismissed the conversation with a snort. His body perked and he looked around.

"You must go. It is getting late," he urged. "Return tomorrow."

"Be careful," Dalka added. "Although your species may be smaller than us, they are very smart. I am unsure of how much suspicion, if any, our presence may have caused. Proceed with vigilance and do not reveal us at any cost."

She dashed out of the clearing as fast as she could, grabbing her book bag. She had forgotten to stop by the house before she came to the dragons and she was filled with dread when she realized her father was home. Ember had lost track of time and knew how quickly her father got angry. It was a costly mistake. She could act like she was at a friend's house, but she soon ditched that idea when she remembered her truck was in the driveway. She knew it wouldn't matter; she wasn't supposed to be out of the house. Regardless of any excuse, Ember knew she was screwed. To add the icing to the cake, she forgot to do her chores, which would make her father even more furious.

She walked in from the back door and tried to be as quiet as possible. Maybe he did not notice that she was gone and—

"*Ember Winters!*" her father yelled.

Ember cringed at her father's harsh, angry tone. He knew of her presence and was royally pissed.

Her mom was not home yet, thus, she had no one to protect her. Ember was on her own. A doe in the middle of a leafless forest, with one very skilled hunter.

Her father stormed from the kitchen to where she had entered. He had a menacing scowl and his hands balled into fists. Although his eyes were blurred by alcohol, she still saw fury, nonetheless.

She could smell the alcohol on him from across the room and knew he was drinking more than normal. She slunk back as he approached her. Again, her focus was on the anger burning deep within his eyes, a fire she had only seen a mere handful of times. She tried to speak and explain herself, but before she could even say a word, her father's face was inches from hers.

"Where have you been, *girllll?*" he jeered at her.

"I uh, thought I saw a dog and went to go find it 'cause I thought it was hurt," she stammered, surprised her panicked mind allowed her to think of a lie with ease.

"Then where is my other gun?" he snapped at her, prodding her harshly in the chest with an index finger. The force of the jab caused her to take a step back.

She'd forgotten about that and cursed herself up and down. With the events that had unfolded in the previous weeks, the gun had slipped her mind.

"When I uh, went out to look for your other gun I dropped, the mountain lion came after me again and I dropped it." She reused the old lie she had used after losing the first gun, knowing her drunken father would not remember her reasoning from the previous incident.

"*You idiot!*" he roared, throwing a punch aimed at her face. His balled fist thrusted forward with more veracity than he prepared for and he lost his balance. He stumbled a step forward in order to stop his fall. Ember jumped out of the way as her father seemed to regain his balance enough to continue his punch. As a result, he punched through the glass door. A resounding *crack* split the air and the glass shattered into thousands of shards, pulling her father out of his drunken rage.

Whether it was the pain from the glass or the look on Ember's face, her father realized what had happened as he stared back at his daughter. The deep cuts to his hand began to bleed profusely and drip onto the white carpet, staining it a deep scarlet as the scent of metal hit Ember's nose.

"Ember...I—"

"Shut the hell up!"

Ember turned and ran out the back door into the woods. She did not go back to Cadell and Dalka, but instead stood a few hundred feet away from the house. She heard her father grumbling and shouting from inside.

She remained for what seemed like hours, but could have been only minutes. Numbness crept through her mind and body. She didn't cry; she didn't feel. She only sat. She only waited.

When she heard her mom's car approach, she sighed in relief but also worried about her mom's safety. She did not dare leave the woods even though her mother had arrived. She heard her mother shout inside and her father yell back before the deck door opened and she saw her mother.

"Ember?" she called. "Ember!"

She refused to come. All she needed was to make sure that her mother was safe and she then knew that she could leave. She slunk away and thought it was best to go to the dragons after all. She let out a breath and held back her tears as she stared at her mom a last time. She didn't want to live like this anymore. But if her mother did not take action, it was Ember's job to. With one final glance back at her mom, the tears in her eyes spilled onto her cheeks.

"I'm sorry, Mom. I love you," Ember whispered hoarsely. She knew her mother couldn't hear, but she allowed herself to say it as a comfort to herself.

She choked back a sob and took off through the woods.

Ember was not one to give up. She was resilient as well as persistent. But she could not run anymore. Her lungs and her legs couldn't handle it. She stopped, panting and crying. Violent sobs racked her body as the shock over the ordeal finally passed. She was no longer numb.

She could feel.

She could feel everything.

It was a crushing, black weight. A demon taking her insides and claiming it as its own. It's all she could feel, it felt like all she ever would feel, and all she had ever felt.

She cried for her mom, she cried for herself. She even cried for the dragons at times.

Ember remembered when she had cried when her dog had died. But looking at what she felt now, it didn't even compare.

She had never cried like that before and nothing prepared her for it. She had no idea what she felt. Was it anger, fear or confusion? Maybe a mixture? She didn't know, and she did not have the energy to put her finger on it.

When the sobs died down to hiccups, she stood and wobbled. She leaned up against a tree and heard something fall out of her pocket. She bent down to see what it was, and almost toppled from a weight on her back. She thanked her lucky stars that she had forgotten to take her book bag off at her house.

When she looked down, she saw her phone. She picked it up and fumbled with it in her hands.

"*My phone,*" she thought, "*Oh! My phone!*"

An idea popped in her head and she immediately dialed 911. Her mom needed help. If her mom couldn't do it, (or rather, wouldn't) then Ember was going to do it for her.

CHAPTER

4

Ember found Dalka and Cadell in the clearing quietly talking. When she approached, they walked quickly over to her looking worried and perplexed

"Are you okay?" asked Cadell, taking Ember by surprise with his concern. "Why are you back so early?"

"I am not going back home," Ember sniffled. She closed her eyes and looked away as tears threatened to spill out of her still burning eyes. "My father...he tried to hurt me. I don't want to go back home anymore. I'm done; there isn't any way I can take it. I called the police and told them my mom was in danger, but did not state who or where I was. I have made sure that no one can track my phone, so we do not need to worry about them finding our location. They are going to search for me in the woods. My mother knows that's where I would run off to. We have to leave before you are discovered."

"He didn't hurt you, did he?" Cadell snarled whipping his tail angrily. He then suddenly seemed taken aback by his sudden burst of anger. He gave a confused look but quickly dismissed it with a shake of his head.

Ember shook her head. "No, he missed. He was too

drunk to swing straight."

Dalka walked over and bent her large head down to Ember. "I'm truly sorry, Ember. You won't have to deal with him again." She closed her eyes and sighed. She allowed her head to hang a moment more near the girl. "Come, before we leave here, Cadell and I want to show you something that we discovered."

Dalka bent down and picked Ember up gently by the back of the shirt and placed the girl on her back. Ember, still shaken up by what had happened, did not fight the dragon. She realized from the time that she had spent with Dalka that the dragon would not hurt her. Dalka looked at Cadell after making sure Ember was settled and she motioned with her head for him to follow. They entered the woods at a fast pace, Dalka's muscles flexed beneath her with purpose as her long strides covered ground. Ember looked behind her sadly and watched the clearing disappear. This place was her home; she had grown up adventuring in the woods. It pained her that she was leaving it behind. She knew that once she left, she would most likely not return.

She knew choosing to come with the dragons had sealed her fate. In that moment of realization, she almost told Dalka to stop and let her off. She thought she could deal with the mess she was leaving behind. But she knew that the dragons couldn't deal with their mess alone. Something deep within her churned but she was unable to muster words of withdrawal from her newfound friends. She felt a lump in her throat and the urge to cry again.

The air was fresh as they walked through the woods. The cold hit her face and she closed her eyes, enjoying it. She embraced the harshness of it, as it almost seemed to take the edge off the pain. Cadell, who had fallen into a steady pace beside Dalka, looked over at Ember. He saw her pain as she struggled to keep herself together. His normally angry and stern face softened slightly at her. He looked away quickly when Ember tried to lock eyes with him.

Dalka arrived at a small pool of water that Ember (knowing the woods very well) knew exactly where and what it was. She found it odd that these creatures found the pool interesting. There must be thousands on the island where they came from. She looked over Dalka's neck and at her face before back at the small pool of water.

"Dalka, I have been to this place many times before," she said. "I told you, these woods are my home."

"I do not doubt your knowledge and familiarity with your homeland," she said before lowering herself to the ground and allowing Ember to get off. The girl walked over to the pool and then looked back at the dragon.

"So?" Ember pressed.

"There has been talk amongst other dragons that the chosen one has a connection with water. I wish to challenge this theory before we leave," she said lowering herself down to Ember's level. "Touch it."

Ember was hesitant, but she pushed past it and took her fingers and dipped it into the water. Gently, she let it slip over her fingers. It was cold and she fought the urge to pull away.

Her fingers began to tingle, it ran up her arm and spread to the rest of her body. It was not unpleasant, but a new sensation that made her uncomfortable.

She looked down at the water and saw an image beginning to form in it. The dragons gathered from behind her as she tried to make out what the image was. She saw a white dragon, a beautifully crafted crown rested on its head, sparkling with diamonds that reflected the light of a setting sun. The dragon sat on a cliff, gazing over a land that was cut off by the end of the pool.

"Who is it?" she asked Dalka and Cadell.

"Our queen," Dalka breathed, "Amrendra."

"She is so...beautiful," Ember said, withdrawing her hand from the pool. The image faded away with the ripples of the pool. She turned around to face the dragons who were shifting restlessly.

"We must leave. I have an idea where we can go," Dalka stated while bending down so Ember could climb upon her.

Ember heaved herself onto the dragon and expected her to move forward at a walk again. But before Ember knew what was happening, she heard Dalka holler at her.

"Hold on!" The dragon called back.

She felt her stomach lurch as Dalka took off into the sky. She gripped hard with her legs and grasped the nearest spike in front of her and squeezed her eyes shut. She felt like the world was spinning and as if she would fall. Their ascent felt like it took forever, but as Dalka leveled, Ember slowly opened her eyes up once more.

"I'm sorry," Dalka called, her words almost swept away by the roaring wind. "I didn't have a choice; I knew you would refuse."

Ember felt angry at the dragon and only nodded. She hadn't found her voice quite yet. *Thanks for the warning.* She thought sarcastically. As the trio flew, Ember slowly relaxed and began to enjoy flying. Heights never bothered her, just the fact that the only thing separating her between an 8,000-foot drop was tons of living flesh. She shuddered, after thinking of the outcome.

As if sensing this fear, Dalka called to her once more. "You're safer up here with me than you would be in any of your human transportation machines," Dalka said. "We call them human death traps, but you call them cars and trains."

Ember brushed the last part off and continued to watch the land below her pass in a blur, the steady beat of Dalka's wings being the only thing that kept time as the sun set.

· · · · ·

Ember didn't remember falling asleep, but when she awoke, she was in what looked like a barn. She was nestled within a pile of hay. She rubbed her eyes and saw Cadell and Dalka below her. Looking around, she realized that she was in a large loft. The air was warm and she was comfortable.

"You are awake," Dalka noted, not turning her gaze from the door.

"Yeah," she yawned. "Where are we?"

"We're in a place your kind calls 'Mexico'," Dalka replied.

Ember's gaze widened. *That's a long way from Montana,* she thought, looking through a small window. She saw that the sun was rising. *They must have flown all night to get here.*

"One of the only humans who knows of our existence lives here. He is one of very few that isn't a threat. He has been kind enough to help out and is harboring us. His name is Jack," Dalka explained, seeing Ember's puzzled expression.

Ember stood up and stretched, her stomach rumbling. She looked down and saw that her bag had been placed next to the pile of hay. She dug through it, pulling out a crushed granola bar. She scarfed it down and pushed the wrapper in her pocket just as the door opened.

An old man lumbered through the door, he looked up at the dragons and smiled before looking over at Ember.

"Ah, so you're up," said the man, his voice laced with a very heavy Irish accent.

He lumbered over to the ladder that led down to the main floor of the barn, his wooden cane smacking the floor as he walked. He climbed up to meet her, tucking his cane under his arm. After he made it to the top, he put out a gnarled hand and shook Ember's. His hands looked more like bear paws compared to Ember's small smooth ones.

"I'm Jack, it is nice to meet you. The dragons came to me late last night. I am sorry I didn't have enough time to prepare something better for you. You are welcome to come inside my home and wash up. I just made breakfast and the coffee is brewing."

Ember looked at the man. He appeared to be around eighty, and he did seem pretty nice. The dragons trusted him, so Ember decided he wasn't a threat. Although it went against everything that she had ever known.

"Thank you, it is nice to meet you too. I'm Ember," she replied with practiced kindness.

"A beautiful name, Ember," Jack said climbing back down and turning back to the door. "Come, come! Your breakfast is getting cold!"

Ember climbed down and walked over to Dalka who smiled and nodded. Cadell was asleep, she could tell from his deep snores. She stood a moment, watching the dragon's sides heave up and down with each breath. Looking away, she followed Jack. The first thing she noticed was the heat that hit her. The ground below her was a mixture of dirt and sand. She looked around and didn't see any other houses, only trees and a few mountains rising in the distance. The sun was peeking over top of the mountains, casting light on her and the house in front of her. It was a small log cabin, but for an eighty-year old man, it was perfect.

She saw Jack standing in the doorway motioning her.

"Come on Miss! I'm 91 years old and I'm walking faster than you are!" he called.

He must have seen her puzzled expression and laughed. "Don't look too shocked, I may not look or act like 91, but I most definitely feel it." Jack called, "Better close that mouth before you catch a fly."

Ember snapped her mouth shut abruptly. The home was small, she came into a small living room with a couch, a couple recliners, and an old wooden rocking chair in the corner. A small old-fashioned TV stood on a cedar dresser, playing a black and white Western movie. The cabin was small, yet cozy and welcoming. Jack closed the door and led her to the kitchen where the smell of bacon and eggs made her stomach growl. That granola bar had done nothing to feed her hunger.

The kitchen was similar to the living room, following the same older country fashion. A wooden table with matching chairs was the centerpiece of the kitchen, made from perfectly carved oak. An old wood stove sat tucked in a corner while a white refrigerator sat next to it humming away loudly.

Jack got down two plates and glasses and served them both a healthy portion of bacon and eggs. He then got a jug of milk out of the refrigerator.

"So, where you from?" he asked pouring the milk into the two glasses he had pulled.

"Montana," she replied bluntly.

"Well that's a ways," he chuckled.

Ember said nothing as she scarfed down the food and drank the milk greedily. When she was done, Jack was only part way finished.

"If you would like, I can start you a bath. I do have some clothes you can wear. They may be a bit big, but they will do until I run to town and get some new ones for you."

She stood up and raised a brow at him, nodding her head down to the dishes. A silent, but universally understood question. Jack pointed to the sink.

"They can go there. Let me finish breakfast and I will get your bath started." he said.

She placed her dishes in the sink and sat back down. Out of boredom, Ember traced the lines on the wooden table, lost in thought as she tried her best to comprehend what had unfolded in the previous 24 hours.

"Will your parents be worried?" Jack asked suddenly, causing Ember to raise her head back up to him.

It aroused unwanted emotions within her. The strongest of them was anger, and it slipped her tongue before she had time to leash it.

"Is it any of your concern?" she snapped.

The old man looked hurt, but he did not say a word. He lowered his head and continued to eat. He looked so sad, but yet seemed so happy to have company. She wondered if he was the only one living here. The thought exited quickly when she felt guilt flutter in her chest.

"I'm sorry, it's just...I really don't want to talk about my parents right now."

"It's quite alright," Jack said lifting his head up, offering a small smile. "I understand."

They made small chit chat after that until he finished his meal and put his dishes in the sink. He motioned her to follow and led her through the halls to a small bathroom. He started the water for her and left for a moment, returning with a flannel shirt and jeans.

"These used to be Martha's, my wife's," he said sadly. "She was never an average woman. Always wore my clothes over the dresses that others would give to her, she was something else. I haven't seen these clothes in over 20 years. She kept on stealing my clothes until I finally went to town and bought her some like my own."

He set them on the sink before turning to her. "Take as long as you would like," he said turning and closing the door behind him.

Ember took her torn and tattered clothes off, putting them in a small pile. Her old jeans had been worn thin on the thighs and inner legs from the long flight on Dalka and her shirt was covered in mud from the woods. When she looked at herself in the mirror, she saw the dirt that smeared her face and how tangled and matted her hair was. She scrunched her face up in disgust at how she looked, embarrassed that she had met Jack that way without realizing it.

Turning to the water, she dipped her feet into it, wondering if it would turn into an image. She still had a lot of unanswered questions about her powers, and as the dragons did not know much about them, they were no help. When the water did not change or do anything unusual, she sat down mostly relieved that she could keep one normal part of her life. She settled down in the tub of water, washing off the dirt from her body and allowing herself to soak in the tub for a while. Her aching muscles began to unwind and she could feel the burning tension fade away. As she sat in silence, her mind began to wonder.

Is my mother worried about me? She felt a familiar lump in her throat. *I don't know anymore; I feel like everything I know is now gone. What has happened to me?*

She allowed some tears to flow before she clenched her fist and punched the side of the tub, grinding her teeth angrily as she did so. The impact of the wall stung her knuckles, but it did not crack her skin. Her vision blurred and she closed her eyes as more tears slipped down her cheeks.

"Enough, Ember!" She yelled angrily at herself in a hushed whisper. She opened her red eyes. "You're stronger than this! Do you really want to go down in history being the weak one?"

When she was finished, she dried herself and put on the clothes Jack had given her. They smelled of flowers and potting soil. It was a very gentle and soothing smell. They were big like Jack had expected them to be, but Ember decided they would do. When she walked out of the bathroom carrying her old clothes, Jack was sitting in a recliner in the small living room.

"Put your old clothes by the door in the back of the kitchen," he said turning to look back at her. "The washroom is back near there; I will wash them after a while."

Ember did as she was instructed, placing the clothes in a stack neatly by the door. She looked inside the washroom and saw that a humble washer and dryer sat in the corner. Returning to Jack, she was about to sit down before he spoke.

"Come, let's go to the barn to see your dragon friends. I have missed them. It has been a good while since I have seen Dalka," he said rising from his seat.

"You know the dragons?" she asked him.

Well, obviously you idiot, why do you think they brought you here?

"Yes," chuckled Jack. "Come, I will explain everything."

Jack took her to the barn and pulled out an old chair from among the things scattered about. With the doors now open and her mind awake, Ember was able to observe the old building where the dragons had taken refuge.

It was an older wooden barn, with a few stalls where some cows, a donkey, and a sheep were snorting and shifting uneasily. They eyed the dragons, the whites of their eyes showing. Across from the stalls, Dalka and Cadell sat quietly watching the two humans and the animals intently. They were nestled on a thin bed of hay. She supposed that Jack had kindly put it out for them.

The back part of the barn held farm equipment and many odds and ends. Car parts, horse harnesses, totes, containers, mouse traps, Ember even thought she saw a Christmas tree in the mix. Looking up, she saw the ladder leading up to a hayloft where she had woken up.

Ember sat in the chair while Jack preferred standing.

"Dalka! How have you been, my friend? I didn't get to properly talk to you since you came in late last night and this young lady did indeed need to be washed up and fed," Jack said hobbling over to the dragon.

Dalka bent her large head down to the man and looked at him with kind eyes. "Not very good I'm afraid, Jack. There is a disease that has struck our island and has killed most of us. This is why Ember is here. She should be able to help us, if the prophecy has spoken correctly. She looks promising, however, and I have great faith in her." Dalka said glancing over at Ember with a kind smile.

"Prophecy?" Jack asked genuinely curious.

Dalka quickly told Jack the prophecy she had explained to Ember only a few weeks earlier. Jack sadly patted Dalka's cheek. Ember could see he was completely comfortable with the dragons. Ember was alright around them, but she still got intimidated by their large size. Jack looked over at Ember before hobbling near the center of the barn, so he was able to see both Ember and the dragons clearly.

"I feel like you want to hear how I got to know them," Jack said, looking at Ember.

Ember thought he was going to tell her his story regardless, so she just nodded in agreement.

"When I first moved here with Martha, we were both in our early thirties. We came from Ireland, and it was our dream to have a house in the middle of nowhere. We wanted to live off of the bare minimums. I had grown up similar to that, out in the country with my father. My mother died during birth, so it was just me and him. My father was not a good man, he was abusive, wicked, and cruel. I grew up fast, learning to take care of myself and unfortunately, my father as well.

"Martha, however, was opposite of me, and almost completely so. She lived in the city with a family that loved her and had enough money to give her anything she wanted.

But she was never happy. The money that they had never brought her any happiness. She loved nothing more than to ride horses or go hiking through the woods. However, her family frowned upon that, and tore her down, stuffing her into the mold they had created for her. But Martha was too strong willed and stubborn to be what they wanted. When she met me, we both knew we were meant for each other. It truly was love at first sight.

"We got married and fled; we wanted a life to ourselves. No families to hold us down, we knew we would be free. That's how we ended up here. It was one night after we had recently moved that we heard something crash down out in one of our backfields. We figured it was someone trying to steal the cattle or the sheep, so I went out there, and Martha of course came along, no matter how hard I tried to keep her in the house.

"When we went out into the field, we saw a small dragon. He had crash landed in our field and ripped his wing. He was too young to be away from the other dragons, but he wanted to be independent just like every kid wants to. Unable to fly, he would have been killed if someone else had found him. His name was Zimmeran, and boy did we learn a lot from him.

"He was mentally around four years old, but we soon learned later he was over 200!"

"Since dragons age differently, we grow up much slower," Dalka interrupted. "Around fifty human years is equivalent to one dragon year. It is a similar concept to that of your canine companion years. One human year, isn't it, equivalent to seven canine years?"

"Dog years," said Jack approving the explanation Dalka

had given. "Anyways, he was still quite young. But he was such a bright and friendly fellow, he was a dream to have around. We took him in and helped heal his wing."

"What color was he?" inquired Ember.

"He was beautiful, exact same spike color as Dalka's—."

Dalka interrupted, lost in thought, "His scale color was a deep red, just like his father's, and you were right about the spikes and horns. Zimmeran had my spikes and eyes. He had similar markings as his father's, but not as pronounced. He had white spots everywhere on him, even on his spikes and tummy. His claws were black, just like his fathers. He was so handsome."

Ember noticed the far-off look in Dalka's eyes. She seemed distant and sad.

"Did you know him?" asked Ember looking up at her friend.

The question caused Dalka to lower her head and tip it down to the girl. "He was my son."

"Now this is my story, can I continue, please?" Jack asked, exasperated.

Everyone nodded and Jack continued with everyone's attention.

"Zimmeran stayed with us for around five years. Since he was still young, we taught him more then he taught us, but we still did learn a lot from him. Martha and Zimmeran formed a bond like no other, you never saw one without the other. Zimmeran was Martha's shadow, and I have lost count of how many times I had to carry Martha from the barn back to the house after she had fallen asleep with him. Sometimes, when Martha had to go out of town for a couple of days, Zimmeran would cry and cry for her. It was really a sad thing to watch.

"Martha couldn't have kids, we tried so many times, but it never worked. Martha wanted children so badly, and so did I. When Zimmeran came down, it was everything Martha ever wanted. Zimmeran was her child, and no one would tell her otherwise. He even took to calling her 'Mommy'."

"Dalka, being the real mother, finally found him. It took everything in our power to convince her we had not done her son any harm, and she finally trusted us. She took Zimmeran back to the island, and they would come and visit us every couple of years.

"It tore apart Martha to see him go, and she changed on that day. But she always understood it was unsafe for him to stay with her. All she wanted was what was best for him, so she let him go.

"Around 25 years after Dalka had found them, they were both flying over to see us, but before they could get here, a plane shot Zimmeran down. Dalka was able to get him back here, and we did everything we could. Zimmeran died in our arms."

Ember saw Dalka lower her head and close her eyes, and she swore she saw a tear slide down Jack's cheek. Cadell sat emotionless, listening to the whole story.

"You see, Ember, your people did us harm too," Dalka said bitterly. "They have done it many times before. He was not the first, and he will not be the last."

"I'm sorry, Dalka..." Ember said.

"After that, Dalka still came to see us, but not as often as before, it just wasn't the same without Zimmeran," continued Jack. "We continued to live here until Martha died in her sleep. We don't know why, or how, but I woke up and found her like that. My lover of almost 50 years, torn away from me in one night. After that, it has just been me."

"I'm sorry for your loss Jack," Dalka said. "I was going to ask where Martha was. It has been a long time since my last visit and I have been away longer than I have liked. I suppose I lost track of time."

"It's been a while, Dalka," replied Jack, nodding. He focused his attention on Cadell who was sulking in the corner of the barn. "So, who is this?"

"Who are *you*?" snapped Cadell, angrily.

"Well then, I can see he is not very nice," Jack said stepping away. "Well, I am Jack. I thought Dalka would have told you?"

"I don't care about your name, you stupid human, why are you important? I don't want to waste my time on an unimportant being." Cadell growled.

Dalka whirled around, teeth snarling and snapped Cadell's wing roughly. She took her tail, hitting him harshly upside the head. Ember knew Dalka was really angry, as these weren't the light and playful hits she did back out in the woods.

"Shut up, Cadell," she snarled, deadly serious.

"But I—"

"Shut up," Dalka said.

She let go of his wing and grumbled, making her way out of the barn. Cadell shook himself, drops of blood flying from his wing and head. Ember wasn't surprised. With the force Dalka used, it was no wonder blood was drawn. Concerned, Ember addressed the black dragon who was busy attending his wounds.

"You alright?" Ember asked Cadell.

"Yeah, what did I say?" Cadell grumbled.

Ember too grew aggravated at the black dragon. "Really Cadell? Are you seriously that self-centered? I am very surprised it took Dalka this long to finally snap at you. You have no regard for how your actions affect those around you. Your ego is so large, that I can't believe it fit through that barn door!" Ember snapped, "If this is what you're going to be like, I don't want you as my partner."

"Fine then! All you are is a weak human with the intelligence of a frightened deer. You would run right into the hunter's bow! You're meaningless to me. We can solve our problem without you or your help!" Cadell roared, striking and breaking a crate close to him with his tail.

The crate splintered everywhere. Flying broken pieces of wood flew and one landed directly in Ember's leg. She gasped and cried out, falling back as the pain ricocheted up her leg. Jack ran over to her, yelling.

Ember leaned her head back and yelled out in pain. The piece of wood was sticking out of her leg, and around it the jeans were turning red, the blood being absorbed by the threads. Blood began to pour from the wound as Jack quickly jumped into action. He grabbed a towel hanging from a stall door and ripped open the jeans with his pocketknife.

He grabbed a hold of the piece of wood and looked up at Ember. "It's not in too deep, but I have to pull it out, you ready?"

Ember didn't have time to respond, Jack yanked the wood piece from her leg and she yelled out in agony, the scream piercing the air around her and scratching her throat. Jack quickly pressed the towel to the wound and bandaged it with some wrap he had found.

"There, that will hold it till we get inside so I can care for it properly." Jack said.

Dalka ran in after the girl had screamed and saw Ember on the ground and the splintered crate near Cadell. "What. Did. You. DO?" snarled Dalka angrily shaking her head and lashing her tail around. Her eyes narrowed as smoke bellowed out of her nostrils.

"It...it was an accident!" stuttered Cadell. "I didn't mean to Ember, I'm sorry."

Dalka seemed shocked at Cadell's apology, making Ember swallow the retort she almost spat at the temperamental dragon. She figured if Cadell did not apologize often, then his apology must have been genuine. She closed her eyes, breathing out of her nose trying to put herself in her dragon's shoes in order to rein in her anger. She thought about how Cadell had been witnessing his whole race die and was currently in dangerous lands trying to find a cure. She decided to forgive the dragon, lifting her gaze up and putting a smile on her face.

Ember got to her feet slowly with the help of Jack. "It's ok, see? I can walk." She said walking in a small circle. "I'm sorry too; we are partners. I shouldn't have said that to you."

The event made her realize that now wasn't the time to fight. The dragons, she now understood more readily, had a temper and could hurt her more severely than what had just transpired. She knew that from now on, the rest of the journey had to be regarded as high priority and navigated with caution.

Cadell grumbled, which Ember took as she was forgiven.

Jack led her back to the house, allowing her to lean on him for support. She could walk, but the wound stung and more tears brimmed from her eyes. When they got inside the small cabin, Jack sat her on the couch and disappeared through a door. He returned with an aged first aid kit and began to clean her leg. The stick was enough to pierce and puncture the skin, but not enough to damage any nerves.

"You were lucky," said Jack as he bandaged her leg. "Dragons are renowned for having a temper. It is best you don't anger them; they could kill you by accident. There were times Zimmeran would get angry and hurt me or Martha."

Ember nodded absently as she watched the old TV.

"You remind me so much of Martha, she was a lot like you," Jack mumbled finishing the wrap and standing, his cane bumping a table as he got up. Nothing fell over, but everything on the table shook slightly.

"Martha never liked strangers. I did all the talking when we went to restaurants and stores. But if she knew you, you could never get her to stop talking. She was a spitfire too. If she was in there with us and Cadell, she would have had his ass on a silver platter above our fireplace, believe me," said Jack fondly.

"You really loved her, didn't you?" asked Ember as Jack sat down in a recliner next to her.

"Yes, more than she ever knew. But she loved me just as much and that's what made our relationship so beautiful," Jack replied sadly. "My nickname for her was Morning Glory, if you have ever seen one, they are beautiful. Martha just loved her flowers. Before she died, the whole front yard was a garden. The day she died, all the flowers in the garden died with her. I'll tell you, that lady could plant anything and make it grow."

Ember smiled, "She sounds like a very nice woman."

"She was, she seemed to make anyone happy if they gave her a chance. I was so lucky to be married to her. I swear sometimes I can still hear her watering the flowers outside, and every now and again a small flower will pop up in the garden, and I am reminded she is still there, and that she always will be."

6

The next couple of days were spent getting adjusted and resting. The dragons flew out and went hunting after the first day and returned the day after. At the house, the old man had a spare room where Ember slept comfortably and had her privacy.

Jack took Ember to town and got her some new clothes with the little money that he did have. Everything went smoothly except for when they went to buy a phone charger for Ember's phone.

Ember saw a pair of men wearing all black come into the store where Jack and Ember had been shopping. When the pair approached the counter to buy the charger, the two men shoved the cashier out of the way.

"We are here to make sure that this hasn't been tampered with," one of the men said.

Ember was uneasy as the cashier sat cussing out the two odd men in Spanish. They opened the charger and did something to it Ember could not see behind the counter before handing it back to her.

"It is fine!" one said wearing a smile that seemed incredibly strained. "You are safe!"

Both Ember and Jack had left the store feeling uneasy but brushed it off and returned back home.

One morning, she went out to the barn to see the dragons and was pounced on as soon she walked through the door.

"We need to educate you on how to fly!" Dalka said as soon as Ember entered. After leaving the refuge spot for a day, both dragons came back in better spirits. She had guessed getting out and releasing the stress by hunting must have helped Dalka and Cadell.

"You can't, I don't have wings," Ember retorted. She was being playful, happy that her friend was happy.

"Not by yourself, on Cadell," the dragon huffed. Ember saw that she was not in the mood for games. "Come, he is waiting outside. It's going to be a long session."

Ember could tell that the dragon was eager. She had already placed Cadell outside, and now that she thought of it, she hadn't seen Cadell in the barn when she walked in. Dalka lead Ember outside to where Cadell was waiting. He was sitting, watching the sun rise over the mountains. Over the past couple of weeks, Ember found that Cadell loved sunrises and sunsets, although he would never admit it. She suspected that it would put a dent in his reputation as the tough guy, so she never bothered to ask him. She always found him watching them when she would come out in the morning or during the evening. He seemed at peace; his muscles relaxed as he stood as still as a statue. The only things moving were his heaving sides.

When the duo approached, he turned to face them. He nodded to Ember in a silent greeting and then to Dalka.

"First lesson of riding a dragon, the dragon is always

in control. You may offer your opinion, but at the end of the day it is the dragon who elects what to do," Dalka said. "It is the ultimate balance of trust and friendship. You are putting your life in the dragon you decided to ride upon."

"That's scary to think about; Cadell would kill me," Ember said, looking up at the dragon who narrowed his gaze and drew his lips back in a slight snarl.

"And if he does, then he basically killed the whole island. So, I doubt he will kill you. He will be very careful, right Cadell?" Dalka said looking over at the black dragon. Her gaze was hard, but grim. Ember had a feeling that Cadell wouldn't kill her, but she knew that he would go to great lengths to convince her that he could.

When he did not reply, Dalka swung her tail and swatted him upside the head.

"Right?" she inquired.

"Ow! You have to stop doing that, you old cow! Yes! Yes, I will be careful," he grumbled, rubbing his head with his talons as he glared at the turquoise dragon.

"Alright then. Now that we got that out of the way, let's start with the basics. When you're getting on the dragon it's impossible to get on them if they're not bending down. When they are, you can use their leg as a stepping stool to climb on their back," Dalka began.

Cadell lowered himself down and Dalka nudged her toward him. "Try it."

Ember walked over to Cadell and climbed on his legs, almost falling as he turned to look at her. Cadell chuckled and looked back at Dalka.

"Hey Dalk, watch this," Cadell said using the other dragon's nickname.

Cadell stayed still for a moment before yelling, "BOO!"

Ember yelped and fell off his leg and landed on her back. Cadell couldn't contain his laughter. Dalka looked like she wanted to hit Cadell again, but once she saw Ember joining in, she couldn't help but laugh as well.

Ember realized after they had all calmed down that she had never heard the dragons fully laugh. They sounded surprisingly human as they did. The dragons were not only clear in speech, but also when conveying other emotions as well. The dragons never stopped amazing her. They seemed so human, and Ember was almost certain that they were smarter than most people. She wondered how the dragons even learned all they knew.

"Ok, try that again," said Dalka still giggling.

Ember got to her feet and climbed back up. Cadell stayed still this time and she grabbed a hold of the last spike that ran down his neck before pulling herself up. She settled in and then looked back at Dalka, waiting for more instructions.

"Excellent! Very good!" said Dalka sitting and curling her tail around her feet. "Now when he is running and taking off, bend down low and grip with your knees and thighs. You are more than welcome to hold on to a spike, most beginners do. As you progress, you will find the need will fade. The most important thing to do is keep yourself small and out of the way so he has room to move freely without any limitations."

Ember nodded and bent down low, gripping with her knees and thighs like she was told, but still holding on to the spike.

"Like this?" she called over to Dalka.

"Yes, but put your legs higher, he would hit you with his wings while you were flying if you were like that." Dalka pointed out. Her head tilted and her nose pointed to Ember's incorrectly positioned legs.

Ember scrunched her legs up more. "What about now?"

"Point your toes down," Dalka said to her. "And when you're taking off, look straight ahead."

Ember did as she was told, looking forward and pointing her toes down.

"There, that's it! Now when he levels out you can sit up but keep your legs where they are. Cadell is going to run and take off now, ok?"

Ember nodded looking straight ahead.

"Alright Cadell, go easy on the kid, please?" Dalka asked, changing to a more pleading and quieter tone before looking seriously at the pair. She smiled and grinned, nodding at the eager black dragon before her. "Ok Cadell! Now!"

Cadell lunged forward, taking Ember by surprise as she squeezed her eyes shut, but she remained steady. His powerful muscles moved beneath her; she could feel every movement he made. Cadell began to increase his speed, faster and faster the trees whipped by. He beat his wings and they pushed powerful gusts of air against the ground, lifting them up.

One foot, then five, twenty and then fifty. Higher and higher they climbed until Cadell leveled out. Ember still sat with her body pressed against Cadell's back, not daring to open her eyes or move.

"You can sit up now," Cadell called to her.

She shifted a bit, opening one eye to look around, and then the other. Slowly she sat up, looking around as she slowly relaxed. They were right below the clouds, so close she felt like she could reach up and touch one. Cadell, Ember found, was indeed a steady flight. His body barely moved even when he would flap his large wings.

The wind rushed past her face, but not nearly as fast as when she had first flown on Dalka. Cadell flew at a more moderate pace, but it still felt quite fast to Ember.

"So, do you realize that being nervous was a really stupid thing to put your energy toward?" Cadell asked, turning his head partly to her.

"Well…" Ember said. "It's alright, better than I thought it would be," she admitted.

"Ha ha, see? I didn't get you killed," he teased. "You are such an unintelligent human." His voice grew more serious and he suddenly slowed down. "How is your leg, Ember?"

"Cadell, I told you it was fine. It was an acci—"

"That still doesn't make it right," Cadell stressed harshly.

It took Ember a moment to realize that he felt guilty for it, and it touched her slightly. Her attention was brought back when his tone grew more serious.

"But if it is fine, can you stand on it for a bit?"

"Yes, but why?" Ember asked.

"There is more to the prophecy than you know about."

"What?"

"Let me find a place to land…I am not going to hold secrets from you any longer," he said.

Ember began to worry. She understood that there were some things they may have left out, but why didn't he just take her back to the barn? She bent back down as Cadell began to descend, her ears feeling stuffy from being at such high altitude. He landed gently and folded his wings, lowering himself so Ember could dismount him. When she did, he bent down to her level, a serious expression covering his face. It was unlike the snarky young dragon that Ember had come to know. The seriousness seemed to age the dragon a handful of years, or a couple hundred years, rather.

"There will come a day when the dragons will begin dying. A plague will cover the island and will kill whoever is in its path. A black shadow will come among everyone, and all dragons will feel its wrath.

"Before this turmoil, a dragon with the scales a darker black than the dead of night and markings a deeper red than an open wound will be hatched. This dragon, alongside a human girl named Ember Winters, shall save the dragons from pure and utter extinction. But with this promise comes a price." Cadell stopped for a moment.

"I have heard all of that." Ember said. "Well, besides the black shadow part."

"Dramatic effect," the dragon replied.

"Is that all you wanted to tell me? Why didn't we just go back to the barn?" Ember asked.

"One human and one dragon must give their life out of love. Both lives that have experienced much hurt, but in the end must be pure and give themselves selflessly to others. Then, and only then, will the dragon race be saved..."

Cadell looked at Ember. "That is the real prophecy."

"It's talking about me, isn't it?" Ember said shakily. "But who is the other dragon? Is it you?"

"Not necessarily," Cadell said. "Dalka and I did not tell you because we knew you would make that assumption."

"It has to be though," Ember tried to reason. "I am the

only one here who knows of you and has been through a lot but has still remained pure, or I think I have at least. But who would be the dragon?"

"You're the purest person *I* know." Cadell admitted. "And it sure as hell can't be me. I am the furthest from pure."

"Aww, that's the nicest thing you've ever said to me," Ember laughed, trying to stop her rising anxiety.

"Shut up. Don't get used to it." Cadell threatened.

They fell into silence as Ember reflected on what she had heard. She thought about the life she left behind and her life moving forward.

"I will still help you." she said slowly.

Cadell shot his head up, surprise written on his face from Ember's words. He, however, replaced it quickly with a scowl. "You are a hatchling; you have barely seen what the world has to offer you. You really expect me to believe that you have the capabilities to comprehend this situation?" The dragon bent his head back and laughed bitterly. "You're dumber than I thought you were! I know your kind, your stupid human race. You're all vile liars. I know if it came down to it, you would turn tail and run."

"I wouldn't run!" Ember yelled. She was clearly trying her best to defend herself and was getting flustered. "I would stand and fight."

She took a breath to steady herself before continuing in a calmer tone.

"Am I dumb enough to climb on the back of a conceited dragon? Yes. Dumb enough to lose everything that my life has to offer for beings I didn't know existed? Yes. I am, however, smart enough to know I have nothing to lose."

"Going into life like that is much more likely to get

you severely wounded rather than killed." Cadell said. "It is rather counterproductive."

"Just know I will do whatever it takes to help you guys." Ember continued to press. She felt Cadell's words hanging in the back of her mind like a cobweb, but she brushed it off. "You have my word."

"Sure, I do." Cadell said sarcastically.

"What can I do to make you believe me?" Ember snapped.

"Explain to me what meaning your life holds." Cadell stated simply.

Ember opened her mouth and then shut it quickly. Her mind raced to formulate a response, but it could not do it quick enough.

"Exactly." Cadell said.

It surprised Ember he did not rub it in that he was right. In all normal occasions, he would have done that. She puzzled over it for a moment before shaking her head.

"Alright. You win. For now." Ember replied, feeling defeated.

Cadell only smirked, giving Ember a smug look before lowering himself. "Dalka will be rather livid, but she will deal. I didn't want to keep secrets. It's exhausting for me keep it from you when you're around." He grumbled.

However, Ember knew deep down that there was more to that statement than he let on.

CHAPTER
7

After Cadell and Ember had returned, Dalka was indeed mad. But, just like Cadell predicted, she was happy that Ember knew everything.

"I'm sorry I did not tell you sooner, Ember," Dalka said lowering herself down to the girl's level. "I hope you unders—"

"I do understand, Dalka," Ember interrupted, not wanting to hear her excuses. "Though, I am still a little hurt by it."

Dalka closed her eyes, a gentle puff of smoke trickling out of her nostrils as she breathed a sigh. "I know, I know. I am sorry."

"It's not that I am angry at the prophecy," Ember said as she gently placed her hands on either side of her friend's face. "It's the fact that you didn't trust me enough to tell me when I am basically putting my life in your hands."

Dalka opened her eyes, pushing her forehead against Ember's for a moment before pulling away. "I am incredibly surprised you would do that," Dalka murmured, "but I can assume you understand from what Jack has told you, our relationship with humans has been a bit *strained*. I was hesitant even coming to meet you."

Dalka backed away from Ember, settling herself in the pile of hay Jack had set for them in the barn. Ember walked over to an old chair and sat down, looking up at Dalka.

"I was very hesitant to come," Dalka repeated, her voice hardly above a whisper, or as close to a whisper as a dragon could come. "I was afraid as soon as I saw you, I would kill you. Your kind killed my son, and I was worried I would be angry with you. But as soon as I met you, my mind changed. You were so scared of us, and so small," Dalka mused. "You reminded me of a hatchling."

"Hey!" Ember shouted, offended by the comparison "I am so tired of being looked down on, metaphorically speaking, by you and Cadell! I am 17 years old, almost 18!"

Dalka laughed. "It's your size my dear, not your actual age. But as I began to learn about you and your species, I couldn't help but become very intrigued. You see, you and I aren't so different."

"What do you mean?" Ember asked.

"You will find out in time my friend," she said gently.

Ember sighed in aggravation. She hated it when people kept things from her. She averted her eyes to the door of the barn as Cadell came from the outside. He nudged it open with his broad snout and folded his wings to fit through the door.

"And where have you been?" said Dalka looking over at the other dragon.

"Merely stretching my wings," the other dragon replied.

"Our trip wasn't enough for you? We flew for a while," Ember pointed out.

"You call that a trip? Silly human, that wasn't even enough to be a warmup!" Cadell scoffed.

Ember ignored that and instead glared at Cadell. "Well, since you and I are partners, why didn't you take me with you?" she said. She enjoyed flying and wanted to go out again.

Cadell laughed. "A human couldn't handle the speed I was going. I have to be careful while you are upon my back, one wrong move and..." Cadell lifted his talons up to his head before dropping them back down to the floor while whistling, adding a "splat!" at the end for effect. "Human alive...then human dead."

Dalka snarled at Cadell, raising her tail at him.

"Okay, okay! I went a little far that time," Cadell admitted, "but that was still funny..."

Dalka whacked him with her tail. "Cadell, you fool!"

"Ow! Dalka!" Cadell whined.

Ember just stood laughing at the two dragons. "You fight more than a married couple!"

"And that's saying something! You know how many fights me and Martha had over the years?" said a raspy voice from behind.

Ember and the dragons turned to see Jack with a carton of eggs and a jug of milk.

"I just came to tell you I am back from town. I forgot milk and eggs last time we went," Jack explained, "but there is also something I picked up that you might want to see."

Ember, Cadell and Dalka followed Jack as he turned and walked out of the barn. He approached his turquoise truck, setting the jug of milk and eggs on the rusted roof before opening the door. He retrieved a rolled up newspaper from a box in his passenger seat and handed it to Ember. She unrolled it and saw her face staring right back at her on the front page.

Missing: Ember Winters

"Must be my mother," Ember said. "Well, at least she still cares for me."

As Ember read on, it was said that an anonymous caller made a 911 call reporting a domestic violence situation. When the police came by the house to investigate, the couple assured them that everything was fine. They said that nothing was wrong. They explained that their teenage daughter was angry and ran away after they punished her when she was not supposed to be out of the house because of a recent incident. Her parents assumed she was the caller and was trying to get them sidetracked so she could run away.

"They lied…" Ember whispered. "They *lied*."

Anger gripped her body like nothing she had ever felt. She ripped the newspaper and threw it on the ground as tears sprang to her eyes. She quivered and stormed into the house, not heeding the calls from behind her. She slammed the door behind her and stood a moment, debating whether or not to turn back. Deciding against it, she made her way to the room Jack had given her and collapsed on her bed in a fit of tears.

Sobs racked her body; she was angry and scared. She didn't know how to let her feelings show in any other way. Ember heard Jack knock on her door a few times but refused to get up and answer. She was too embarrassed by her behavior to muster up the courage to do so. Ember sat sprawled out on her bed long after she got done crying, looking up at the ceiling. She thought back on everything that had happened and why her life had been changed so quickly. Ember wondered if maybe it was karma for something that she had done that she didn't remember. She really was clueless. She had a hard time believing things would get better. The only thing she wanted was everything to go back to the way it once was, even if her father remained a drunk.

When she felt like she could get up without breaking down, she opened her door and walked out where Jack sat in his recliner. It was dark outside now. Jack, instead of watching TV like he normally did, sat facing the wall. When he saw her approach, he lifted his gaze. He seemed tired, as if he had been waiting all day for her.

"I am guessing what I read in the paper wasn't true then?" Jack said peering up at Ember.

"No."

"Would you like to tell me what happened now?"

Ember sighed before sitting down on the sofa and bringing her legs up and tucking them beneath her.

"My father was a very good salesperson. He was so good, in fact, he was constantly on business trips. But other than him being away a lot, my family was happy. We had money and we all loved each other, and everything was great. But suddenly, a jealous coworker turned on him, feeding lies to the board committee about things my father didn't do...or so he claimed. He was fired and was forced to take a much lower-paying job. I was eight when my father lost his job; he started drinking and every year he got worse and worse. He used to drink once a week. Then it was once a day, until I never saw him at home not drunk. He said he felt most normal that way. But he failed to realize how *not* normal it was for us. My father is oblivious to how his actions are affecting others, and he is in turn tearing apart our family.

My mother is either too blind or too stupid to see what is happening around her. So, when I left the house to go with the dragons, I called 911 in hope that with them there she would finally 'fess up and they would both get the help they needed. I just want my mother to get the support that she deserves." Ember stopped, looking down at her hands. "But that proved to be wrong, as you have read in the paper. They have no idea about the dragons and I plan to keep it that way. I am just so unbelievably angry that my mother, of all people, would be the one to betray me." Ember looked back up at Jack, her eyes cold and tense. "You now know why I didn't want to tell you. Some things are best left where they came from."

Jack's expression drastically changed. His expression, once kind and open turned angry and stern within a matter of seconds.

"And you think that it was easy for me to tell you my past?" snapped Jack. His voice was sharp as steel. "If you would take a step back from yourself for one moment and look, you would see you are not caring for those around you, just like your father."

This struck Ember like a freight train, a bullet to the heart. Now she knew. She looked down and reflected.

The time she snapped at Cadell, when she was being the same way, yelling at Taylor, leaving her mother...dodging Jack's questions and wallowing in her own self-pity. All this time she failed to see it; she was just like her father.

But she wasn't him, she would never be him.

Never.

"You don't get to compare me to my father," she snarled at him as she struggled to defend herself. "Not you or

anyone else! You have no right, no right at all, old man!
You have no idea what he has done to me or my mother!
You do not get to judge me, no one does! Yes, I may have
done some wrongs and I will admit that. You've pointed
them out, good for you. But comparing me to my father
has crossed the line, many of them in fact!" Ember stood
up and without looking back, she went across the living
room and walked out the door.

Ember stormed out of the house and found her way into the barn where Dalka and Cadell were consumed in a conversation. They looked toward her as she entered. They waited to hear the reason of her arrival at such a late hour.

"Are you alright, small one?" Dalka asked when the girl remained quiet. Ember saw the dragon was hesitant, as if she knew that Ember could lash out.

Ember shook her head, too angry to speak her thoughts clearly. She knew that saying a word could expel a waterfall of things she didn't want her two friends to hear.

Cadell gave Dalka a look as if he couldn't care less.

"Go on, Cadell." Dalka ushered.

Cadell scrunched his face in disgust. "What do you mean 'go on?' I am not her taxi driver."

Dalka snarled and lifted her tail. "Is the avoidance of getting smacked good enough pay?"

Cadell grumbled under his breath. "Alright, Runt." He huffed as he pushed past her to go out the door. When she did not immediately follow, he glanced behind him and drew his lips in a snarl. "Well? Are you coming along or not?"

"I don't think I like your tone." Ember said, crossing her arms and glaring at him. "I am not coming along unless you say 'please'."

"This ain't my ass I am trying to calm down." Cadell snarled. He lowered his head to look Ember in the eyes. "I will happily stay here."

"Cadell!" Dalka spat.

Cadel rolled his eyes, huffing in defeat. "Please?"

"That's better." Ember smiled. She then turned and followed him out the door. "So, where are we going?" she asked.

Instead of responding, he continued to lead her to the spot they had been that morning. He bent down and looked over at Ember.

"Keep yourself small and out of my way. You made me sore because of this morning." Cadell instructed.

Ember scrunched her nose and shot the dragon a glare. "I mean what do you expect?" Ember asked. "I have never flown on your back before."

"I wasn't looking for justification. I was merely telling you something." Cadell snapped. "Just get on. I don't have all night."

Ember climbed on without hesitation, eager to get away. She was not going to let Cadell's sour mood ruin it for her. She positioned herself the way Dalka taught her. However, this only resulted in Cadell accidentally hitting her leg with his wing as he took off. He let out an irritated snarl but did not say anything. For once, Ember was grateful. She scrunched her legs up more, realizing they were down too far. He leveled out, but instead of slowing down and gliding like last time, he flew faster, pumping his wings to take in more air and push him faster.

The wind blew past Ember's face, tossing her hair behind her. The pressure of the speed pushed down all around her and it made her forget everything. While flying, she forgot all the pain and worries she had. She loved it.

She opened her mouth and laughed, grinning as Cadell went faster. He angled his wings downward in a sharp dip, causing Ember's stomach to drop and her to laugh more. He rose back up to the height they once were and angled his wings so that he could go farther up. After a few more minutes, he slowed down and began to glide. The wind stopped rushing around her and it was quiet once more.

Ember pushed her hair out of her face. Not entirely caring at the moment whether or not she fell, she took the chance and lifted a hand in order to do so. When her breathing and Cadell's evened out, the dragon broke the silence.

"Look down," he said. He lost the anger in his voice, and instead almost had a tone of amazement to it.

Ember looked and she gasped. She hadn't been paying attention on what was around or below her. She was more focused on the feeling she got while she was flying. They were above a city, thousands of lights illuminating the sky below them. She could see the skyscrapers and the smaller buildings that shadowed them. They watched the cars that were now incredibly small navigate the city below her like a maze. When the lights below dwindled and became sparser and far apart, the view faded off into the faint outlines of trees, lightened by the moon.

"They are beautiful," she said.

Cadell didn't answer. He banked slowly, circling the city below him. They stayed and admired the lights for a few moments more before moving on. Cadell picked up speed once more, clearly flying with purpose to a destination he had in mind.

The stars shone brightly above the pair, and the moon cast a gentle glow upon Ember's skin and Cadell's scales. The moon kissed the dragon and girl as they began to descend. Cadell's wings shifted to allow him to cut through the air smoother as he slowed. He landed gently on the side of a cliff that showed the city off in the distance and gave a clear view of the night sky. The beauty took Ember's breath away.

After lowering himself to the ground and allowing Ember off his back, Cadell turned to face her with a gentle look.

"Why are you mad?" Cadell lowering himself so that Ember would place her attention on him and not on the beauty behind him. "Did the old man do something? Must I kill him?"

Ember chuckled and Cadell gave her a rare smile. She saw him do a 180° since she met him. She wondered why he had loosened up so suddenly.

"No," she said as her smile receded back. "He just said something that hit a nerve and he was right."

"What did he say?" the dragon questioned, a bit of venom in his voice.

"He called me out on a lot of the things that I was doing. I didn't realize I was projecting on the people around me, just like my father did with his drinking problem."

"But you have not done anything your father has done," Cadell protested. "Though have you thought about why he might have said that?"

"I did say some mean things...I need to apologize to all of you guys for how I have acted," Ember said, coming to a realization.

"You haven't done anything to me," said Cadell, tightly closing his blue eyes. "I'm...I'm sorry as well."

Cadell shook his head and smoke leaked out of his nostrils.

"Damn, that was hard," Ember said mockingly.

"Shut up."

"I think you have grown soft."

"Don't tempt me, kid."

Ember laughed and the dragon settled down next to her and looked out at the stars. Ember leaned her head against the dragon's shoulder and she could feel him tense up. She waited a few moments in case Cadell reacted violently before she fully relaxed. She was still used to his unpredictable behavior. Even though it was fading, she kept an air of caution. But when he did not, Ember relaxed. They sat in silence for how long, Ember did not know. Then a question popped in her head.

"Did you always now you were the chosen one?" she asked.

"Why do you ask?" He snarled.

"I am curious." She replied.

"The less you know the better." He growled.

"Please?" Ember asked.

Cadell breathed a sigh. "I knew I was different, and everyone knew something was off with me. I looked nothing like my parents; I mean my sire was blue and my dam, grey. I wasn't predicted to look like I do."

"Many of the elders made the connection that I was

similar to the dragon described in the prophecy. It was a rough revelation to my parents, but I never really thought differently about it. There was nothing bad happening on the island; the plague had not arrived yet."

"How old are you?" Ember asked curiously.

"1,324 years. We measure time the same as you humans do."

"Geez! You are old, Cadell!"

"I am not! Stupid human," Cadell growled. "For you humans maybe, but in your years, I am about 26. Anyway, the plague didn't arrive until about a year or so ago.

"Many of the young dragons that I grew up with found it fun to look down on me because the elders always called me 'the chosen one'. I currently believe they must have been jealous of the attention I was getting from the greatly admired dragons. I, being young, did not see this and would always get angry and lash out. I didn't want to be seen as the weak one always on the bottom of the pecking order, so I became mean. I found that an easier and less shameful position.

"I bullied others that were lower than me, and still do. I have a hot temper; I am mean. I know that it is wrong, but I put up so many walls that it now seems normal.

"Since many of the traditions and hierarchy in our race rely on prophecy and fate, leaders are born looking like leaders, kings are born black like me, except for the red markings, and white like you saw Amrendra. My dam and sire called me unfit to take up position as the next king after I had exploded and became rash. I was being trained to become the next king and I was supposed to be mates with the current queen, Amrendra. But since my parents saw me not worthy, they went to the elders and they stripped me of my position.

"After that my anger continued to rise. Instead of trying to earn back my position, I continued to lash out. I blamed what had happened on those that bullied me. I became friends with dragons that would also help me put down others. They, similar to me, were tired of being on the bottom, so we became known as the Rebel Dragons. We did things I am not proud of and deep down I always knew what I was doing was not the right thing. I constantly had a voice in the back of my head saying 'Stop!' and that I was 'Better than that,' but I never listened. I thought that listening to it would just make me unhappy and ridiculed even more than I already was.

"I got into so many arguments with my dam and sire that I left their cave at a young age and have never seen them since. Now older and wiser, I realize that what they did was the right thing to do. I don't even know if they are alive. There are so few dragons left on the island. At this point it is just a small portion of our clan and stragglers from others that joined us. I guarantee if I was leader, we would all be dead by now.

"Amrendra is doing a good job leading what little remains of us on that torn up island. I give her credit, she and her righthand man Jasso are doing a great job. I can't wait for you to meet the other dragons. They will all love you."

"If I even make it that far," Ember said.

Cadell's eyes dulled as a deep growl erupted from his throat.

"Nothing is going to happen. Quit your worrying, human." Cadell said tightly.

"Making promises you can't keep isn't worth any of our time," said Ember.

"Are you doubting me?"

"No. I am saying that none of us know what will happen in the future. Everything is unknown right now and saying that things will or will not happen shouldn't be done."

The dragon stayed silent and Ember began to shift through the new information that she had received about Cadell. What he told her made the way he acted seem much more reasonable. She didn't realize that her new friend had been through a lot, and it made her heart hurt to think about that.

And then her mind wandered over to Dalka.

No amount of pain could ever equal what Dalka must have felt losing her child. Both dragons watched their race die in front of them. Ember could not even fathom how traumatizing that would be for any being.

With a small sigh, Ember closed her eyes and stopped her mind from thinking about it anymore. It was making her upset.

Ember yawned as Cadell looked up at the sky. Ember saw him looking at the position of the moon before he turned back. She guessed that was how they told the time.

"Come, let us fly home. It seems you are tired," He said. "and I am tired of being a shrink."

Ember scoffed and looked up. "Yeah. Thank you, Cadell, this really helped me."

Cadell didn't reply, but he bent down and allowed his friend to climb upon him once more.

CHAPTER
9

Ember had fallen asleep on the ride back on Cadell's back. When she awoke, she was tucked against Cadell's warm belly and next to Dalka. The two were talking but they didn't realize she had awoken.

"...if she can't," Cadell said in a hushed voice.

"She is going to have to do something. The others will kill her," Dalka said calmly.

"Let them try and touch her," Cadell growled quietly.

"You against twenty other dragons? You know I would help you, but we would all be killed," Dalka replied, eyes downcast. "I doubt she will allow them to resort to violence though. I have hope things will unravel correctly. As the humans say, it is how the baked dough treat crumbles."

Ember had to bite back a laugh as Dalka attempted to use the term she had taught her.

"We can tell her they would love to meet her to keep her mind at ease. I don't want to worry her; it will make it harder for us to get her to the island." Cadell quietly stated.

"And there we go hiding things from her again," Dalka replied. Her voice did not hold anger, but rather a shameful tone.

"I know." Cadell said.

"You care about her, don't you?" Dalka mused.

"No!"

Dalka only chuckled and they settled into silence. Ember chose that time to make herself known. She stirred and opened her eyes.

"Welcome back, small one," said Dalka, gently amplifying her voice from its original whisper.

"Thank you," Ember said stretching. "What time is it?"

"Three o'clock in the afternoon," Dalka replied.

"Well, I slept late. Where is Jack?"

"In the cabin," Cadell piped in. "Why don't you go in and groom yourself?"

Ember nodded and stood. Yawning, she walked over to the cabin where Jack sat watching the old television set. She could see the bags under the old man's glasses. His white hair was a mess on top of his head, and he still had the same clothes on as the night before.

Ember stood in the doorway for a moment debating on what she wanted to say.

"Jack...look. I am..."

"Don't apologize," Jack said holding up a hand. "We both did wrong; I should not have blown up like I did. So, I am sorry."

"I'm sorry too," Ember said somberly.

"It happens, my girl. We learn from it and move on," he chuckled. "Lunch is in the microwave and a new change of clothes is sitting on the sink in the bathroom."

"Thanks, Jack. I don't know how to repay you for all that you have done," Ember said.

"You don't need to repay me at all," he said. "Now go

eat and wash up."

Ember ate the sandwich from the microwave and washed up in a better mood. She was happy to get rid of the straw pieces within her hair and the dirt from under her nails. When she got changed, she grabbed her phone which had charged in her room. She had it turned off in the bag for most of the time, but when she got the charger, she was able to use it and turn it on. There were over a hundred missed calls from all of her friends, mother, and employer, but she swiped them all away. She kept the phone to be in touch with the outside world. It made it easier to check new articles online and see what was going on in civilization. It was just a precaution; she was able to see how much disturbance she and the dragons had caused. She shoved it in her pocket before going out to the barn to talk to the dragons. When she entered, she saw how upset and distraught the dragons looked.

"Hey, is everything ok?" Ember said entering the barn.

"Hold on, child," Dalka said, not really paying mind to the question.

"I think the best course of action is to stay in the mountains for a while," Jack said.

"Damn it," Dalka snarled.

Smoke bellowed dangerously from her nostrils. Ember wondered if fire would follow suit.

"Guys?" Ember looked at the dragons and the old man.

"There is an organization that knows about dragons. They call themselves PFIB, People For International Balance. They are disguised as a helpful organization, but they are one nasty and vile group of people. Their main goal is to locate and kill any dragons that they see or hear of. They, however, do not know where their island is. Which is a good thing considering they would probably have already wiped out the dragons. The people that are in the organization know the dragons exist, but they are doing all they can to keep anyone from figuring it out." Jack explained.

"Why does this matter?" said Ember wanting Jack to get to the point.

"They are nearby and they must know we are in this area." Jack said.

"How did you find out they were here?" Ember asked.

"A friend of mine," Jack stated simply. "Me and him have been friends for years and we made an agreement where he would warn me if he saw them. Remember Ember, this is not the first time I have had a dragon in this barn. Somehow, they caught wind that the dragons flew here."

"We tried to fly high on our way here, but some human must have seen us." Dalka said bitterly. "Stupid humans don't seem to know how to keep their noses out of other's business."

Ember and Jack remained quiet, not wanting to tick off the dragon any more than she already was.

"Do they know that you guys are here?" Ember asked. "Like, at this exact location?"

"I don't know. But if they realize you are with us, they will be tracking you intently," Dalka said. "If they catch you, I don't even want to think what would become of you."

Cadell snarled next to Dalka, showing his displeasure.

"Dalka, Cadell, go hunt and stay high in the mountains. You can see if anything happens from there. Ember, stay with me. If they come looking for the dragons, you can hide in the stalls with one of the animals," Jack said. He held a high tone of authority and confidence in his voice as if he had been through all of it before.

"But doesn't the government know of them? Wouldn't they help us if we asked?" Ember asked anxiety clawing her stomach.

Jack's expression was downcast. "No. They wouldn't understand what to do. None of them have ever seen or heard of the dragons, and the legal things that would go with it would be insane. I would think they would arrest me and you, then take the dragons away for testing. It wouldn't end well unless a large majority of the public knew about them the way we do. If that happened, there would be so much outcry that the government would have no choice but to oblige their wishes. However, that is not an option or a risk we should take. It could go terribly wrong if people were afraid of the dragons." Jack paused what he was saying to look over at the dragons.

Both dragons seemed even more visibly distressed and Ember's heart longed to comfort them.

"I won't be able to keep Ember safe if I leave. I am not willing to leave the key to the island alone," Cadell said, standing by this decision.

Ember's heart sank a little bit. She had hoped that the time she had spent with Cadell had made them closer. *Does he really only think of me as the key to the island?*

"Cadell, you can't do that," Jack warned. "You have my word I will not let any harm come to her."

Cadell seemed to consider the deal for a moment. "Alright," he sighed. "But if anything happens, I am killing you first and then all the others. My race will not die because of your stupidity." He lowered his head and puffed smoke in Jack's face, fogging his glasses.

"That is a threat," Jack said coughing and removing his glasses to clean them.

"No, that's a promise," Cadell said with no hint of amusement.

Dalka snarled at Cadell. "Now is not the time."

Cadell shut up quick, and Ember could see he sensed the severity of the situation and felt how tense the air was around them.

"Go," Jack urged them.

The two dragons nodded, and Dalka bent down to Ember. She placed her hand on the dragon's nose as Cadell walked out of the barn. Ember looked into her eyes for a moment, silently wishing they didn't have to go. "Promise you will come back?" she pleaded.

"Yes," Dalka said. "Stay safe, little one."

Then Dalka followed her friend out the barn door and Jack and Ember followed to watch them go. Ember swore she saw Cadell glance at her, a hint of worry in his eyes. They pushed off, sending dust and sand into Jack and Ember's faces. They coughed as they watched the dragons fly low over to the mountains. Ember stayed until they faded off far from sight and she could no longer hear the beating of their wings.

CHAPTER

10

There was nothing the old man and teen could do except to wait in fear. Ember was not sure if the cavalry of PFIB officials would come knocking on the door of the cabin, and this made her very uneasy. She took to pacing in front of the TV to pass the time while Jack sat calmly.

"Stop pacing!" he chuckled. "It is not going to solve anything."

Ember shook her head. "I am too nervous to stand still."

"That is how Martha always was. In these situations, all she did was walk around or clean. She just needed to get her mind off of things before she went mad dwelling on them."

Ember listened, but didn't reply. A cat sat on a deer head hanging above the fireplace and lazily watched her, oblivious to the dire situation. Jack stood up and hobbled over to the window.

"Go to the barn, Ember," he said.

"What?" she said, panic rising within her chest.

"I said *go!*" he shouted. "Hide in the stall with the cow; she won't do anything. Just get behind her and bury yourself in the hay."

Ember turned and opened the door, darting out into the old barn. She did not dare look up the lane. She saw a Jersey cow standing in the stall and it looked at her when she approached. Ember quickly grabbed hay and threw it in the stall, taking a few trips to get enough in so she could bury herself. The cow did not seem to mind the girl's presence and moved over to let her in. Ember buried herself inside the pile of hay and curled up as tightly as she could.

Ember turned off her phone, not wanting to take any risk of it going off. She also did not know when she was going to have access to a charge again, and thought it the best option to save the battery. She knew even with the phone off it would drain power. It would not last longer than a handful of days.

She peered through a crack in the stall. She could see the driveway that led to the cabin. She saw nothing. Wondering why Jack had told her to come in the barn, she was now contemplating leaving. But she suddenly heard the faint *thump, thump, thump,* of a helicopter fast approaching and engines roaring down the gravel driveway. Confused and scared, Ember saw black vehicles fly down the driveway.

"FBI! We have a warrant!" she heard voices shout.

"Hand up! Hands up!"

"You are surrounded!"

She squeezed her eyes shut as she tried to determine voices. She could hear Jack's a few times, but the continued shouting drowned it out. Ember was well aware the men outside yelling about being the FBI were lying. It was a good way to fool those who did not already know of PFIB's existence.

The animals that were once calm began to snort and cry out. She felt the cow move onto her hand and jerked it away as the bovine crushed it. She bit her other hand to help hide the cry that threatened to escape.

"Where are the dragons?" She heard a bitter voice yell.

"Dragons? What do you mean?" Jack replied.

"You know exactly what I mean." Another voice piped in.

"I do not." Jack snapped back bitterly, venom dripping from his voice. "If I were you, I would take your men and your dogs back where you came from. I don't know what the hell you are babbling on about, but you're insane."

Ember heard scuffling and wrestling outside, followed by Jack shouting angrily and the men beginning to argue with him.

"Get off me!" Jack shouted.

"Not until you tell me where the beasts are!" said one of the soldiers.

Her attention was pulled when she heard dogs barking outside. Her heart sank as she knew they would smell her. Even with all the different scents in the barn, these dogs were bred to sniff out people in situations like this.

She heard the barn door open and people step inside.

"FBI! Anyone inside come out with your hands up!" a man's voice shouted.

It echoed through the barn causing animals to call out and the cow to moo. She heard things being moved around in the barn, metal clanking and glass breaking. She hated hearing all those things of Jack's being destroyed and she felt guilt mixed with the panic.

"Look at all this hay on the floor sir," said a man whose voice sounded like a young adult. "It looks as if he was covering a large area so something could sit."

"Something like those wretched beasts," snarled a man near the stall where Ember was hiding. "The man knows something. He is just too stubborn and stupid to say anything."

"Yet Captain Penser," the younger voice questioned, "you, I mean, we all work side by side with one of those 'beasts,' but you still don't like them?"

"It is part of the job. If it wasn't for that thing, we wouldn't have the death toll we have now," the other voice replied. "It's lucky that they are so stupid. We just have to keep dangling false hope in front of its nose until the rest of them get killed off. After that, he will join the rest of them in hell."

Working side by side with one? Death toll? Ember thought, staying as still as she could, barely breathing. *What could this mean? Is there a dragon that betrayed the rest of them? But why? Why would a being turn against their own race? Who could be so heartless?* Ember grew sick at the thought. She didn't want to think about it.

She heard the sniffing of dogs in areas around her. One stopped by her stall and began to bark but the trainer pulled it away.

"Come on, Rocky! It is just a damn cow."

The dog whined but followed his trainer. Seeing that there was nothing in the barn, everyone left and Ember sighed in relief.

She let her muscles unwind and her stomach calm down. She felt sick the moment she heard the chopper. With a few deep breaths the nausea faded and she felt relief spread through her body.

The animals around Ember, however, did not seem at

ease. They all snorted and sniffed the air; something had made them upset.

"It would be best if you just got out of the hay, girl. I will not hesitate to pull this trigger," a raspy voice said.

Ember's breath hitched. They had found her.

She slowly raised out of the hay, holding her hands far above her head so they could see she was not armed.

"There you go. Aren't you that girl missing from Montana?" the man said, surprised at this revelation.

Standing out of the hay she was able to get a view of the person.

He was wearing a black shirt with a bullet-proof vest over top with black jeans and black glasses. He was holding a large gun which was pointed at Ember. He looked at her over top of the glasses with steel grey eyes, as if daring her to do anything. His pose ready, similar to that of a stalking lion.

Looking down the barrel of the gun, Ember's throat swelled in fear, but she managed to swallow the tears and look the man in the eyes.

"I am not armed, so will you please lower the gun?" She asked as calmly as she could manage, but her voice still shook.

"You never answered my question," the man snapped at Ember. "Answer me!"

"Yes!" Ember cried out. "Yes, I am that girl."

"What are you doing here?" the man asked.

Ember did not answer, unsure of how to reply. She could not say that Jack was her grandpa, as all of her family was dead. It was only her, her mother, and her father. She was certain that they would research Jack and see if he was related to her, and it would show she was lying, creating even more suspicion. Saying he was a family friend was also out the window. They would call her parents and see if they knew Jack, and they did not. Saying anything about the dragons was a big no no.

"Answer me, you idiot!" said the man thrusting the barrel of the gun at her chest.

"I ran away, okay? And the man helped me!" She stuttered.

"Do you know anything about the dragons?"

"No," she answered.

"Fine then," the man said, still holding the gun on her. It was cold, and it hurt from the amount of pressure. "You have till the count of three."

Ember squeezed her eyes shut, holding her breath and tensing her muscles. She knew if she fought, he would just shoot her then and there, but if she continued to lie, she would be killed. But she was not going to give the dragon's cover away.

"One...two...thr—"

"Penser!" a voice cried out from outside the barn.

"Not now!"

"Penser!"

"I told you not now!"

"PENSER, MOVE YOUR ASS OUT OF THAT BARN!"

The man didn't have time to react before the barn exploded around them. Where Ember saw the hayloft and part of the roof, she now saw the sky as Cadell ripped angrily through the barn like it was paper. The barrel was removed from her chest and a deafening roar sounded.

"GET OFF HER!" Cadell yelled angrily. The man

stumbled backwards, tripping on pieces of wood that Cadell had broken.

Penser held up the gun, aimed it at the girl and pulled the trigger. The dragon had already stepped in front of Ember and the bullet only bounced off the dragon's scales and flew out the barn where a cry was heard.

Cadell bent his large head to Penser. Smoke bellowed out of his nostrils and he puffed it at the man's face, causing him to cough harshly.

"Touching the girl was a bad idea," the dragon growled as his markings began to glow. "I would suggest leaving before I decide to kill you."

The man stumbled backwards away from the dragon, not taking his eyes off the large creature looming ominously above him, casting light with his strange markings.

Before Ember could fathom what was going on, she was picked up by one of Cadell's talons as he took off, keeping her close to his underside. Ember saw Dalka flying with Jack alongside Cadell.

She heard gunshots going off behind her and thousands of clinks all around her. That was when Ember realized Cadell had her beneath him rather than on his back. He was not keeping his stomach exposed, and was rather flying at an angle so they could not shoot it. Ember was completely guarded all around.

It was not the most comfortable feeling being gripped by the talons of a dragon, and it was scary not having anything below to stop her if the dragon were to let go. But something told Ember if the dragon was willing to rip apart a barn in order to reach her, he would not be keen to make a simple error by dropping her.

Ember lost track of time as she watched the trees go by fast below her. She heard the rushing of air go past her ears and being moved by the pair of dragon's wings as they flew over the mountain. The air began to grow colder the higher they climbed. As if sensing she was cold, Cadell began to descend. He landed on the other three talons before gently placing Ember on the ground. He gingerly nudged her and sniffed her, looking her over.

"Did they hurt you in any way?" Cadell asked as Dalka landed beside him with Jack.

"No," said Ember shivering. "But they now know that I am affiliated with you."

"Did you tell them anything?" Dalka questioned looking at the two grimly.

Ember shook her head as Jack began to talk.

"No, but breaking through like that and retrieving us now shows them we mean something to you. They will now start to target us. They can get us to lure you or to hit a nerve," Jack said leaning heavily on his cane and Ember was surprised he was able to grab it in the fray.

"Did you have a better idea?" Cadell snarled.

Dalka sighed. "I know. But I was not willing to let anything happen to you two."

"I couldn't have cared less about the old man," Cadell muttered.

Dalka snarled at Cadell. "Shut it, hatchling."

"Why didn't you kill that agent?" Ember asked. "I feel like that might have saved us a lot of trouble and time later on down the road."

"I didn't want to do that in front of you," Cadell growled. "You couldn't handle the sight of that."

"Now isn't the time to play parent, Cadell," Ember argued. "I don't really give a damn if I couldn't handle it or not, but I don't want us to be hunted down for the rest of this trip because you care about my mental health."

Cadell's stare turned cold and he lowered his head down to the girl. "You better listen here, Ember. *I* don't really give a damn if you think you're ready or not. I know for sure that you are going to see plenty of things you don't want to. I know that you could not handle me killing that man. To add to that, there was no reason to kill him. I had saved you, and with hope he may get the message and not mess with us again."

Ember was about to yell again before Jack gave her a look of warning. She shut her mouth, and changed the subject.

"Guys," said Ember trying to stop the argument, "I heard something in the barn that I think you should know."

"Go on," Dalka urged.

"I heard them talking about 'beasts,' which I can only assume was you since they asked me if I knew about dragons. That didn't surprise me as much as them saying that they were working alongside one."

Cadell's and Dalka's heads shot up in surprise. "What?" they asked in unison.

"That's as much as I know. That and a death toll. They said if it wasn't for the dragon, they wouldn't have the death toll. They also said they were baiting it with something only to kill it off once the rest of you were dead. I don't know what it means. The agent that had me cornered was named Penser."

"At this point anything will help," said Jack. "We are now on their radar, which is not a good thing. We have to be incredibly cautious now. Anything can give our cover away."

"Then, what are we going to do?" asked Ember, clearly upset. "Where are we going to go?"

"I have a place in mind," Dalka calmly answered. "But it is too early to fly. It is too dangerous to fly in daylight, unless there is a lot of cloud cover to conceal us. They will be monitoring the sky after finding us. We have to stay here for a few days at least."

"I don't want to leave my home," Jack called up.

"There is nothing left for you, old man," Cadell told him bitterly. "They will find us there."

"I need to go back. That's my home," Jack pleaded.

"Let us go back and salvage what we can for him, Dalka," Ember pleaded.

Dalka closed her eyes considering the request. When she opened her eyes, a small puff of smoke came out of her nose and she hung her head slightly. Ember could tell that her request was not something that she wanted to do.

"All right," Dalka said giving in. "But in a few days' time. Let us scout it first and then we will bring you both."

"Thank you," Jack said realising a breath of relief. "I have too many memories in that old home. I can't bring myself to just get up and leave it."

Dalka closed her eyes a moment and then looked over at Cadell who also seemed less than pleased with the development, but he reluctantly agreed with the majority.

Ember was shivering due to the lack of clothing, and she could see that Jack too was starting to grow uncomfortable from the sharp cold air. Ember looked up at the dragons.

"We can't survive here. We are not built for this type of weather like you are," she pointed out. "We will not survive without shelter or warmth." She rephrased the words to add emphasis, hoping the second sentence would convey the necessity for warmth to the dragons.

"We will start a fire," Dalka said turning to go into the woods.

Cadell followed her, and the two humans were left in the clearing.

"How do you think they found us?" Ember inquired.

"I am not entirely sure," said Jack, adjusting his stance to even out his weight. "But my guess is if they found us once, they will find us again. We will need to keep moving. Luckily, the dragons are fast, and incredibly smart. If we let them think it through, then we should make it out alive."

"It is kind of scary to think about. Putting your trust in animals? I mean, Jack, I know they are smart, but I can't help but still see them as an animal," Ember said.

"That is understandable," Jack replied gently. "Just keep in mind they are not so. They are smarter than us, intelligent, but yet have predatory instincts. The perfect blend of human and animal. Capable of killing in just one flick of their claws, and choosing to view the world with intelligence. They are truly something."

"Yeah," Ember breathed. "They are."

11

The dragons had gathered a large stack of firewood and for the first time, Ember got to see them breathe fire.

Cadell stepped back, inhaling a large breath of air, causing his sides and chest to expand. He then exhaled slowly and a gentle stream of fire flew from his mouth, heating the air around him and casting shadows around the clearing despite the bright afternoon sun. Dalka joined her friend, turquoise scales expanded with air before she exhaled a flow of fire, but hers was a bit duller than Cadell's.

"Wow," Ember breathed in awe. "How did you do that?"

"Every dragon can breathe fire," Dalka said. "It is a part of our being; it lives inside us. We just have to reach in and find it."

Cadell who was finishing creating the large fire, turned to Ember.

"I wonder if that's why you have powers with water. Water drenches our flame," Cadell theorized. "When we are wet or in water, we cannot create fire."

"I can't believe I am saying this, but I think Cadell is right." said Dalka, lowering her head to the girl. "There is so much to learn about you, small one. I don't even know where to begin to even start figuring out your powers."

The dragon's deep green eyes closed in stress as she sighed. Smoke gently filtered out of her nostrils making Ember sneeze. Placing her hand on the dragon's nose, the teen tried to remain positive.

"I believe we will figure this out," Ember said hopeful. "We can do this if we work together."

"Fake hope is not going to work here," Cadell rumbled. "Even if the prophecy is real, we may save our race, but there are still a lot we most likely will not be able to save. Who knows how many lives, both human and dragon will be lost. We must realize the situation we are in is dire. There is no use pretending something good will come out of something that will just end up being bitter in the end."

Ember could feel Dalka retract her head to look at Cadell, and she braced for another argument.

"Remaining positive never hurt anyone," Dalka noted coolly.

"Indeed," Jack called up.

"Let's just take it a day at a time," Dalka told the group gently.

The conversation halted and they all settled down by the fire. Ember sat next to Dalka, leaning against the large creature as the warmth radiated from the fire, lulling her into security.

Bending her large head, Dalka touched the cheek of the girl. "Thank you for everything, child."

Ember smiled tiredly. "Don't thank me now Dalka, I haven't done much yet."

"But you came with us, PFIB is now following you," Cadell pointed out. "You could have chosen to stay, we would have never forced you…okay, Dalka wouldn't have forced you. I probably would have tried. But the point is, you went willingly. You are willing. Why?"

Dalka's head remained near Ember as she thought about the one-word question carefully.

Why? Why had she?

"I…I don't really know, Cadell," Ember whispered. "I couldn't tell you why. If it was anyone else, if it was anything else, I would have said no. I would have never dreamed I would be on the run from a crazy organization, I never even fathomed I would be hanging out on top of a mountain with two dragons. I thought those dragon sightings were a joke." Ember's eyes began to water as she spoke. "Now, I completely ruined my life by helping beings that I have only known for a few weeks. Even though my father might have made my life hell, I would have been able to make a life for myself," Ember said wiping her tears. "I threw my life away for you guys. So, I either die helping you guys like the prophecy states and pray it's not in vain or I survive. But even if I complete what I am supposed to, I could very much live the rest of my life in jail. Regardless of the outcome, I will be an outcast to society."

Everyone stayed quiet for a moment before Cadell spoke.

"It is unlikely anything will happen to you. What have I told you about worrying about stupid things?"

Ember looked up at Cadell with red puffy eyes.

"You will live with us on the island after this is done," Dalka said placing her head gently in Ember's lap. "You will be well cared for and loved. I promise."

"If I live long enough to get there," Ember bitterly replied.

"The prophecy never states you." Cadell pointed out again, his voice clearly showing he was agitated.

"Yes, but I am the only candidate among us," Ember replied.

"Indeed," Dalka said. "But we will not let any harm come to either of you two. We will find a way."

They fell back into silence again, watching the large fire flicker wildly in the center. There was not much to do except sit and wait. Ember dozed in and out, only getting up once to relieve herself. She was completely exhausted mentally and physically.

She would catch bits of conversations at times. Sometimes they were about her, sometimes they were about other dragons or people, and sometimes she didn't even know what they were about. All that she remembered was closing her eyes during the night and then opening them to find that it was day. She rubbed her eyes and stirred from her position next to Dalka.

"I am glad you are awake, small one," Dalka said peering down at her.

Ember yawned. Not really feeling the need to reply, she pushed herself to her feet. Her stomach grumbled as she looked around the clearing to find Cadell and Jack missing.

"Where did they go?" asked Ember.

"They went to hunt for food," said Dalka, her voice strained as she stretched her muscles. "Jack has been accustomed to these woods and knows the best place to find food."

"Alright," Ember replied as she lifted her arms above her head, unlocking the joints that were still stiff from sleep.

"Ember, I have a question." The tone in the dragon's voice made Ember turn around concerned.

"Yeah Dalka, what's up?" Ember asked looking at her friend.

The dragon shifted uncomfortably. Her head tipped to the side as she peered to the ground. Her behavior was so unlike what Ember knew that it began to worry her.

"Dalka? Did something happen? Are Jack and Cadell okay?" Ember was on the verge of panic as she looked up at the nervous dragon.

"No! No, they are fine." Dalka rushed to comfort the panicked girl. "I just need advice."

Ember let out a breath relieved. "Yeah, Dalk. What can I do?"

"Do you ever feel like you're not important?" Dalka asked almost in a whisper.

"What?" Ember asked shocked. "Dalka, you are so important, to me and to Jack. Hell, even Cadell loves you!"

"I'm not talking about that," Dalka murmured. "I came here with Cadell as a guide, a protector. I know these lands, I understand them. I have navigated them before. But I am not stated in the prophecy. I am only on the sidelines, Ember. I want to matter. I want to do something. I have lost so much; I feel as if I should be able to matter. I want to be looked up to. I want to be admired, but I am only the sidekick."

Ember stood a moment not speaking, doing her best to formulate her response. She decided to take the road that her mother always took when Ember felt the way Dalka did.

"I'll tell you something that my mother always told me." Ember began, sitting down on a dampened log. "Your worth is only equal to the value you have on yourself. To me, Dalka, you are important. I don't get how other dragons won't look up to you. Yeah, Cadell might have the powers, but who had the wisdom? Who kept him under control? Who braved the human-infested lands?" Ember paused allowing this to sink in before she continued.

"It was you, Dalka. Sometimes it is easy to get swept under and feel as if you mean nothing because the others around you are doing great things. Even though Cadell was destined, he was *given* the right more than earning it. You earned the right to come along on this adventure. You lost a lot, yet you learned a lot."

Dalka's countenance seemed to harden into confidence and realization.

"Thank you, Ember," Dalka said, bending down to the girl in a gesture to show her kindness. "I guess I needed that."

Ember laughed. "Sometimes you do."

Both turned their heads as Cadell and Jack entered the clearing. The dragon had a large deer hanging from his jaws and Jake seemed exhausted and red with heat.

"Welcome back," Dalka called to the pair.

Cadell brought the deer next to the fire and laid it down gently before turning to Jack who was still lumbering behind him.

"We would have been back sooner if this crippled human didn't take forever to walk a measly three miles," Cadell spat.

"Well, we wouldn't have taken forever if you would have just let me fly on your back," Jack snapped back.

"You think I am going to let you fly on my back?" Cadell said bitterly.

"You let Ember!" Jack retorted.

"Because I have to!"

"No, you don't!"

"Yes, I do!"

"No, you're just too stuck up and conceited to admit you like Ember."

This seemed to strike a nerve and Cadell bent his head back and growled deeply. "Why you—"

"Enough!" snapped Dalka. Her tail lashed in agitation and her menacing glare was directed at the two males before her. "I have enough things to deal with. Your bickering can wait until we find a more substantial place of rest. Right now, we need to make the most of what we have."

Cadell growled at the command of his older friend, but he submitted and went over to the other side of the clearing, muttering something underneath his breath.

Jack sighed and rolled up his sleeves, coming over to the body of the deer that lay on the forest floor.

"It will be much easier if we go back to my home and get things to cook it with," Jack told Dalka.

Dalka closed her eyes as if trying her best to ignore the pleading request of the old man. It reminded Ember of a mother who was trying her best to keep her patience with a child.

"I understand that you want to return to your home. But we must wait a couple of days to be sure they have left. Even then we cannot be sure. Cadell and I will fly to see if it is clear in a few days. If it is, then we will bring you both back with us. If it isn't, then we will wait."

This answer did not seem to faze Jack and he began working on the deer while Ember turned to look at the dragon in confusion.

"We can't just sit here and do nothing!" Ember said, visibly upset.

The dragon smiled, seemingly expectant of the girl's problem. "We won't be doing nothing. We will be working on your powers."

"How? We don't even know where to begin!" Cadell called from a handful of yards away. "How do we even start something we don't know anything about?"

Dalka's tail swept the forest floor and she replied almost instantly. "What is mysterious can be revealed. The unknown is not necessarily going to be hard to unveil. Let us see what we can uncover."

The smell of cooking meat brought Ember's attention back to the fire. Jack had already gutted the deer and was hanging chunks of meat over the fire on a stick. Juices dripped from the freshly cut pieces and she could see that both dragons were visibly eyeing the food.

"Go and hunt," Ember told her friends. "You have to keep your strength up just like us."

"Well," Dalka pondered. "We have not eaten in a while. What do you say, Cadell?"

Cadell's attention had already been on the two as they mentioned food. He stood and turned to head into the forest.

"I'll take that as a 'yes'," Dalka muttered loud enough for Ember to hear, "Stupid hatchling."

The dragon turned and followed her younger friend into the woods. "We will return soon," Dalka called over her shoulder.

Ember returned to Jack and waited as he cooked the meat. They both watched the flames flicker in comfort even without conversation. Ember broke the silence when her thoughts began to get the best of her.

"Hey, Jack?" Ember asked. She almost laughed as she realized that she was doing the same thing Dalka had done only a little earlier.

"Hm?" Jack answered, not bothering to look up from what he was doing.

"Do you think that we will make it out of here alive?" the girl asked.

Jack hesitated, putting down the stick he was rotating, allowing the meat on it to cook.

"How would you like me to answer this?"

"What do you mean?"

"I mean," Jack stated, "Do you want the sugar-coated version, or can you take the reality that we are in right now?"

Ember closed her mouth abruptly and analyzed the situation before she dared speak. Jack was completely different now. He was once kind and loving toward her at his home. He still had that demeanor, but Ember knew something had changed. He wasn't angry, but she could tell he was visibly stressed and tense, leading him to be ruder in his replies and arguments. She knew that he felt responsible for Ember, and Ember acknowledged that she was not making it any easier on him by asking him that question.

"Tell me the truth," Ember said, swallowing hard.

"I do not know," Jack stated simply, returning his attention back to the meat which had begun to burn slightly.

Ember fell back into silence as Jack took a piece of meat and handed it to her. Ember bit into it and sighed in contentment. The juice splashed in her mouth and dribbled down her chin. The meat was tender, almost perfectly cooked due to many years prior experience. She loved deer meat; it sent her back to the times that she would go out with her father and camp. She shook the thought away, fully knowing the other feelings that would ensue.

Both Jack and Ember ate what they could of the carcass before Jack hauled what they both could not eat to a nearby snowbank. Ember watched as he began to dig a hole in the snow and place what was still edible of the deer inside.

"That should stop the decaying at least a little bit," Jack said noticing Ember's confused stare, "And with the dragons and us around, we can scare off any animal that tries to get to it. "

Ember nodded in understanding as the old man made his way back to where she sat. He clasped a hand on her shoulder and smiled down at her sadly.

"I do not entirely know where we are going to go, or where we are going to end up. But I can promise you that I will not let anything happen to you that is within my control," the elder promised.

That meant a lot to Ember, seeing that he and the dragons were the last things she had after choosing to embark on this journey. "Thank you," she said.

Jack squeezed her shoulder and sat down near her and began to whittle wood that he had gathered with a pocketknife. Ember chose to watch the clouds in the sky go by as she thought. She knew that the silence would be of value to her. This was the time she had to process her thoughts and formulate plans she might not have thought of before.

Occasionally, birds would cry from a tree, and Ember would get distracted and try to guess what kind of bird was behind the call. When suddenly all the birds went quiet and then scattered, Ember sat up and saw her two dragon friends enter the clearing. They had been gone for some time, but returned with no deer or other prey.

"Were you not able to find anything?" Ember asked, concerned by the lack of food.

"Oh no, we found more than enough," Cadell mused as he laid down and stretched. "We just don't eat in front of you humans. You could not handle our eating habits."

Not wanting to test Cadell's theory, she merely nodded and took his word. Ember could tell it was around noon since the sun was almost directly overhead. She was aware everyone was restless, including herself. She doubted that they were ever going to be at ease in the woods, and the dragons would only feel comfortable if they continued to move. While Jack, Ember and Cadell resorted to sitting and taking in the serene sight before them, Dalka took to pacing. She could see Dalka's mind working in overdrive. She didn't seem to notice anything and was lost deep in thought. A dull look came over her eyes and that worried Ember.

"Is she alright?" Ember whispered to Cadell who had settled next to her.

He bent his head down near the girl and whispered to her so his friend would not hear their conversation. "Don't be concerned. She is just thinking," Cadell said. "This is how she copes with stress. Just let her be, it is no use trying to help her."

Ember shook off her friend's warning and stood. "Hey, Dalka?" she called over gently.

The dragon stopped in her tracks when she heard the girl call over to her. She lost the faraway look and gave Ember her full attention. She did not make a sound, but Ember understood that she was giving her permission to speak.

"Why don't we work on my, I mean, my and Cadell's powers? Maybe we can work on that?"

Dalka's face immediately lit up at the idea and Ember smiled. She knew giving them something to work on would not only help Dalka, but it would also help her.

"That is a great idea!" Dalka said, her tail sweeping the ground excitedly. "Come," said Dalka beginning to lead the way into the dense forest.

Ember walked through the forest, and she was struck with the sad memory of the woods that surrounded her home. She missed it deeply. The pair of dragons led her to a clearing.

Ember could see that the turquoise dragon was clearly thinking and planning. Her tail swung back and forth stiffly and she constantly would puff smoke as if she was dismissing ideas she did not deem fit. After a moment, Dalka stopped as if she had found something that suited her needs.

"Try and pick up dirt." the dragon instructed.

Ember did what she was told, scooping up a handful of loose dirt.

"I am sorry about this Ember, but this is a learning experience," Dalka murmured grimly.

"What?" Ember asked confused, now a bit nervous.

"Close your eyes," Dalka demanded.

Ember obeyed, but she began to feel fear. She could not see anything and didn't like not seeing what the dragons were planning.

"Now think. Think about your mother that you left there with your father. Your abusive, demented father. Who knows what happened to your mom, or your friends?

You left that life behind. Whatever happened to them is your fault, Ember. Yours."

Ember's mind raced. Back to her seventh birthday party when her father wasn't drunk, when he was a father, a dad. His laugh piercing the air like crystal, her happiness like a freshly blown bubble. The air light, the mood filled with grace, perfection.

She remembered how she felt. Ember felt wanted, whole and complete. Even with her small family, she knew she didn't need numbers to feel as if she had the biggest family in the world.

She then remembered the time she shot her first deer. Standing in the tree stand with her father, her breath coming out in gentle wisps as she spotted the buck come cautiously into the clearing. His head pricked as if he heard something. His stance widened as if he was ready to run.

"Now!" Ember's father whispered into her ear.

She pulled the trigger before his hot breath even reached her ear. The buck fell harshly on the ground and then the memory turned again.

The memory was suddenly thrown into darkness, fast forwarding to her sixteenth birthday party. The memory turned tainted; it made her feel like a dead leaf that had just caught the spark of a flame. The memories came at her too quickly. Her father stumbling into the room drunk, smashing the cake with his fist, fuming at her mother and her for being too loud. He threw his empty beer bottle at the wall, making it explode into millions of pieces before going to grab another from the fridge. Both Ember and her mother ducked behind a chair and watched as the drunken man exited the room muttering to himself. When he left, her mother put a candle in what was left of the cake and sang "Happy Birthday" to Ember, who was crying too hard to notice.

No.

It was never my fault.

It was his.

How DARE you!

All Ember felt was red hot anger as she was shoved back into reality. She became vaguely aware of the dirt turning to something in her hands. She chucked it at the dragon before picking up another handful, turning it into the stone and hurling it at the dragon again. She was aware that she was attempting to hurt a friend who saved her life just the day before, but she couldn't escape the fury that gripped her mind. Anger was pulsating through her veins, her heart pounding in her ears.

She heard voices telling her to stop, but she wouldn't. They meant nothing to her, she would not be blamed for something she had no control over. She would not have the hell she was living be turned against her. She would be damned before that ever happened. Relentlessly, she screamed obscenities at the dragon, stopping entirely in her tracks as tears ran down her face.

She didn't stop screaming until something picked her up from behind as her hands tried to scoop the air blindly. She had stopped yelling at this point and began sobbing. The tears coming so fast she couldn't see past them. The rage had suddenly turned into sadness and a sense of betrayal. It was hard for her to wrap her head around why Dalka had done what she did.

"Ember, stop it, please," Dalka said from in front of her.

She could barely see the sorrow that was etched deep on the dragon's face due to the tears. Dalka clearly showed the regret she felt deep within.

She saw Dalka's head get close enough to her and she whirled her hand back and smacked the dragon across the face. Dalka's face turned into shock, but she did not react angrily.

Ember was still sobbing heavily as she tried to get a hold of her emotions. It took her a moment to realize that Cadell had hold of the back of her shirt. She could feel his hot breath on her neck and it gave her some sort of comfort that her friend was there. Ember almost told herself she should be mad at Cadell too, but pushed that thought away when she could hear him trying to soothe her between clenched teeth.

He set her down between his legs and lowered his head down to her face, pressing his nose against the girl's tear dampened cheek. He let out a gust of warm smokey air, trying his best in an awkward attempt to soothe the upset girl in front of him. Ember turned and hugged his face and Cadell's eyes opened wide in surprise, but he collected himself and pushed his face into Ember in a silent show of support.

Ember began to calm down. The familiarity and the gentleness of her normally brash friend worked well to calm her. She sat down next to Cadell's large leg and looked at Dalka with bloodshot, angry eyes. She noticed the dozens of Merocomee stones that littered the clearing around them. The highest concentration of them were around Dalka.

"Dalka, that was too far," Cadell snarled, deadly serious from above her.

"Look," Dalka said gesturing around her with her tail. Her voice shook, it was clear that she regretted her actions and was now trying to justify them. "This is more than enough Merocomee to heal the whole island. Just an ounce of it can cure a full-grown dragon."

Around them, dozens and dozens of Merocomee stones sat scattered about the clearing.

Cadell snarled and he stepped over Ember to confront Dalka. He raised his head and looked at Dalka with anger. Ember noticed that he seemed to age years in just a few seconds.

"What you did was *wrong*, Dalka," Cadell said. "It was very, very wrong. You and I both know this. Even with all the wrong things I have done, I still do not make excuses for them. You know how important truth is."

Dalka backed away from Cadell. Her friend's voice held venom and anger, but remained steady and calm. Everything he had done in the clearing, from comforting Ember to challenging Dalka in a level-headed and authoritative manner was unlike him. Ember saw Dalka's face change; she saw the change in Cadell too. This journey had affected him more than they both realized.

"Cadell, look. I just didn't know—"

"Damn you," Cadell snapped. "I never once claimed to be naive about something I knew either. I understand that the situation we are in causes matters like these to be more delicate, but we need honesty."

"I thought it would help. I didn't think it through," Dalka said, closing her eyes and bending her head in shame. "I am sorry."

"Dalka…" Cadell warned.

"I am sorry, Ember," Dalka said peering over at the girl who sat near the black dragon's back leg. "I don't expect you to forgive me after that, but I want you to know I am so sorry and I will do anything to make it up to you. I was rash and stupid. I wanted the best results quickly. I got carried away; I should have thought how it would affect you."

Ember looked down at the ground. She wasn't angry anymore, she felt more betrayed and scared. Dalka's voice blaming her played and replayed in her head.

"I didn't know you blamed me for this whole thing," Ember sniffed.

Dalka's face showed how her heart broke and how the reality of what she had just done hit her.

She pushed past Cadell who snarled but moved.

"Oh, little one, I don't blame you for that. I did that to get you angry. I did not mean that." Dalka stood a few feet away from Ember, not approaching the girl, almost in fear of getting hit again.

"How do I know that you're not lying? Ember said, looking at the dragon.

"You will have to take my word for it," Dalka said. "However, I wouldn't have asked for your advice, or saved you. I love you a lot, Ember. You and Jack are the only two humans I can bear to look at without wanting to tear you apart. You managed to worm your way into my heart, both mine and Cadell's. Not just because you are part of the prophecy, but because you are special and we love who you are."

Ember took that as a good enough explanation. She laughed at Dalka and smiled at her. "I guess I am pretty great, huh?" Ember laughed, her voice still thick from the onslaught of tears. She held out her hand for her friend to come to her. Dalka did not waste a moment and came over to the girl, gently pushing her face into Ember.

When the dragon pulled away, Ember stood and looked at Dalka seriously. "So now that I went through that, was there something for me to gain? Or did I totally screw it up by losing it?"

"No, that was my plan." Dalka admitted. Ember could see her visibly flinch as the words escaped her lips. She knew that she was taking Cadell's advice to avoid another confrontation.

"I wanted you to remember what you felt in that moment," said Dalka. "That power, that overwhelming sense of power will get you very far, or that is my theory."

"Where did you hear this?" Cadell asked. He had been silently observing the two interact from a short distance.

"The elders," Dalka said smoothly. "The same ones who told the prophecy. I remember hearing them talking about powers, but that is something we will have to explore more in depth when we get to the island. I just want to work on what we can be somewhat prepared.

Ember only nodded, still breathless from her explosion of emotions.

"Would you want to try again?" The dragon asked hesitantly. She seemed to know that she was treading on thin ice.

Ember nodded in agreement, but Cadell growled in disapproval.

"Dalka!" Cadell challenged.

"Cadell, enough," Ember said without hesitation.

The dragon shut his mouth and watched her with a terse

blue stare. He let his disapproval show through his features and posture.

Ember closed her fist around the piece of dirt and felt a gentle pull of energy within her. She closed her eyes and called it out. She felt it flow to her hands and out onto the dirt. Suddenly, what was loose soil was a not so pink Merocomee stone.

"Well," Dalka sighed. "With practice it will become purer like those around us. The sad thing is, none of these are usable after a few hours."

"What?" Ember asked confused. A small wisp of anger floated from within her. "You're telling me that I went through all of that for nothing?"

"No. You gained the knowledge of the power that is within you. I also learned a valuable lesson. But about the Merocomee, think about a fruit, Ember. It can only stay good for so long when in contact with air. Merocomee is the same way, except much more sensitive," Dalka explained. "It must be used and synthesized immediately for it to have any benefits."

Ember sighed. How was she ever going to help the dragons? Everything was foreign and new to her and at times she couldn't even wrap her head around it.

"Do you think that I have the power to synthesize it?" Ember asked hopefully, grabbing a pure stone near here. She could already see that it was beginning to grey around the edges.

"No, that is strictly for the healers and the healer apprentices of the island," Dalka said.

Ember sighed and dropped the stone at her feet. She felt disappointed by that lack of power.

"Come, let us not be discouraged," Dalka said. "You have come very far today; we are both proud of you. I think even though that was a short session, it is enough for today.

12

The days following the training session were rather uneventful. Dalka refused to bring up anything about the powers after that and instead went back to pacing, much to Ember's dismay. On the morning of their third day out in the woods, Cadell and Dalka set out to see if Jack's house was safe for them to return.

"We will return as soon as we can," Dalka told the two humans who were still rubbing the sleep out of their eyes. "Stay in this clearing. We are going farther than we did when we hunted. It makes me nervous not being close. Do not do anything that will draw attention to your location."

Cadell who was eager to leave jumped up and flew off. This caused Dalka to end her sentence abruptly. She gave a curt nod to the two humans before lunging into the sky and chasing after her friend.

"I would suspect them to be back in an hour or so," Jack said as he shuffled around the clearing picking up stray sticks that had blown from the trees due to the dragons rushed departure. "They are more eager to leave than we are. They would have only stayed until dark in these woods the first day we came. We would have already been in God knows where."

"Where do you think they will take us?" Ember asked.

"I really don't know," Jack said. "But if there is one thing I know about the dragons, is that they never go anywhere without having at least two backup plans."

Ember stopped to think for a moment; Jack was right. If they had not, they wouldn't have been at Jack's. They seemed to have everything planned out. It was really remarkable how capable they truly were.

"I really don't know much. I only know from what Zimmeran and Dalka have told me." Jack said. "I have always wanted to learn about the dragons, but that isn't something you can just look up in a library or online, you know? I mean, some of the information that is given is correct, but as far as their social structure and hierarchy, there is just too much for us humans to get our head around."

"I understand that," Ember said, agreeing with the older man. "I wish I could find a book that explained them so maybe I could find out how to use my powers, and what powers I really have. I mean, I know I can do things with water and dirt, but what else?"

"I don't believe that any of the dragons know the full extent of your power," Jack said thoughtfully.

"Dalka said something about the elder dragons talking about it. She said that when we got back to the island, we would meet up with the elders to find out. I am just worried that whatever is killing the dragons will kill all of them before I get there." Ember said.

"Ember, I believe there is more to this than you are seeing." The old man said.

Ember scrutinized her friend. "What do you mean?"

"I mean that there is more to saving the dragons than just clearing the plague. Yes, discovering your powers and healing the dragons will help them in one area, but now there is another problem we have to deal with. I don't know if the prophecy even spoke of PFIB. If PFIB finds the island location, I fear they will kill off all the dragons before the plague does. There are only so many dragons left now," said Jack.

Ember's heart sank as Jack spoke. She knew he was right. "We cannot give up hope," Ember said. "I don't care if you do, I don't care if Dalka and Cadell do, but I will not."

Jack flashed Ember a smile and brushed back his frizzy gray hair. "That is my girl."

They both sat near the dying fire in silence, waiting for their friends to return. When they heard the beating of wings in the distance, it was Jack who was the first to stand. The two dragons dipped and landed in the clearing with practiced ease before folding their wings and looking at the two expectant humans.

"It is clear, let us not waste time," said Dalka bending down next to Jack.

Cadell walked over to Ember and allowed her to get on. Jack got onto Dalka, and while it looked like he had done it before, it made Ember wonder if he had. When both the humans were settled, the dragons took off and began the journey to the house.

The elevation change made Ember's ears pop and suddenly going from cold to hot made her feel sick. She pushed the undesirable feelings aside and watched the scenery go past, happy to leave the clearing. She was aware of everything around her, checking the sky above and looking at the ground below for any signs of something that could harm her or her friends. After around 45 minutes of flying, they began to descend. She knew carrying her and Jack on their backs, the dragons could not fly as fast. Thus, it made their flights longer.

They landed on the ground gently, lowering themselves so the humans could get off. Ember looked around her and her hand flew up to her mouth in shock. Everything was destroyed, broken, or burned. Ember looked over at Jack who was surveying the wreckage with a solemn expression. He did not, however, seem shocked.

"Jack," Ember murmured. "I am so sorry. This is all my fault."

"No," said Jack shaking his head. "I knew that it was going to happen sooner or later."

He sighed and picked up something from the ground. When Ember looked closer, she realized it was the antenna from the old TV in the living room.

"To be quite frank, Ember, I think this was for the best," Jack said.

"Wait, what?" Ember looked at the old man, more shocked by his reaction than the devastation at hand. "Why?"

"There are too many memories in this house. All I ever did was sit in that living room before you came. There was really nothing for me to do, all my friends are dead, dying, or unable to remember me. My family is gone, and so is Martha. I got a new life, a new meaning to life when you came along. That house, although it holds great memories, serves no purpose now except to remind me of the memories which are now gone."

Jack paused his speech for a moment and set down the TV antenna before picking up a brick. It was broken, worn away and crumbling. But it still managed to stay together in his hand.

"It was time for it to go."

Ember stayed quiet and listened to the old man. She could tell he was sad, but she knew he was right. It was never too late for new beginnings. She let him explore the wreckage of his home alone, feeling it was a personal time for him. She stayed back with the dragons who too watched Jack sift through his broken things. He only looked through the wreckage for a few moments before returning to them with a broken picture frame. Inside, she saw a picture of Jack, who she believed was Martha, and a small dragon that fit the description of Zimmeran.

"This is what I came for. I didn't really have hope that it would still be intact," said Jack as he shifted it in his hands. "This is the only photograph I have of Zimmeran. I can't believe that they didn't come across it."

Dalka, hearing her deceased son's name, came over and looked at the photograph. "He looks so beautiful," she whispered, her eyes shining sadly.

Jack took the picture out of the broken frame and put it into his shirt pocket.

"There were no food or clothes for me to gather; everything was taken or stolen. I hid this picture in an old shoe box, I don't think they even bothered to check it and see that I had lined it with metal so it wouldn't burn."

Ember took a last look around at the charred remains of what once was Jack's home before turning to the dragons who sat silent. They too did not know how to react, but Ember thought she knew they were probably acting the only way they knew how. Seeing that they had witnessed the death of most of their entire race, they must have been through a lot of trial and error in trying to help and comfort others. They must have settled on silence being the universally accepted and go-to answer for devastation.

The dragons lowered themselves to the ground again, giving the option for the two humans to get on their backs if they wished it. Ember chose to get on the back of Cadell, but Jack stayed a moment longer and looked out onto the horizon. With his charred house demolished, Ember could now see the faint outline of the city. Ember watched as he breathed deeply before turning around to get on Dalka's back.

"Let us rest in the clearing until nightfall. We will then depart to a friend who will harbor us," Dalka told the humans when Jack settled on.

"How long will it take us to get there?" asked Ember.

"Well, with no one on our backs it would only take around three hours, but with humans it will take around six," said Dalka.

Both dragons stood and adjusted themselves to fly. With a glance back to their human companions, they launched into the sky and began to make their way back to the clearing. The way back was silent, and it allowed Ember to reflect on what she had seen. It made her heart hurt to see Jack's house so torn apart and broken. She wondered if it really affected him more than he let on, and she was sure it did.

She had this deep feeling in her gut that it was her fault,

and the guilt that she felt really hurt her and made her sick to her stomach. Her anxiety began to increase and she closed her eyes in an attempt to stop it from rising. She inhaled a breath of air and realized that it had changed back to cold as they climbed higher into the mountains.

The dragons went at a faster pace, clearly eager to get back to the clearing and rest. Ember, however, longed to stay on the back of her dragon friend; she knew that once she got back to the clearing she would sit and overthink everything. Seeing how Jack's house was destroyed made her worry more about how others who were involved in the journey would be affected. Ember didn't want anyone else taking them in after what had happened to Jack. She already caused a lot of devastation for the old man, and Ember didn't think her heart could take anything bad happening to someone else. When the dragons got back to the clearing, she heard Jack curse and looked to see the source of his distress.

All around the clearing were the fur, bones, and meat of the deer they had hunted a few days prior.

"I knew that was going to happen," he said as he slid off Dalka. "Damn animals."

"It looks like we will have to go hunting for some more then," Cadell suggested. "However, I think it is best you let me go this time since you can clearly not keep up. We need to be quick about what we do now."

Ember could see that the old man was clearly agitated by the snappy dragon, but he chose to keep his mouth closed in order to prevent conflict. Ember heard Dalka growl in warning from behind her as Cadell turned and flew off to hunt.

Dalka turned and lit the dead fire as Jack went around

the clearing picking up the scraps the animals had left. Ember watched the two in silence, wishing that there was something for her to do to keep her mind busy. She took a stick and began to draw in the dirt. She looked at Dalka and began to do her best, sketching the dragon out in the earth below. She was no artist and knew her skills were the same as a child's, but she wanted something to do.

She started first with Dalka's head. It was smooth and defined with horns coming out where ears on a normal animal would be. She had bright green emerald eyes with a smooth muzzle. But when the muzzle opened, it revealed rows of bone-colored teeth, reflecting the light and warning of their dangerous nature. It then dipped to a deep broad chest plated with big, flexible scales. Her legs were shorter but bulky, allowing for landing and taking off when the dragon flew. Her stomach was broad and barrel-wide, heaving when air rushed in and out. Dalka's tail was long with spikes running down the middle until it forked off to allow for steering while flying. The tail also doubled as a weapon when needed. The dragon had a long back with spikes running down it, an obvious defense from long ago when a predator attacked from above. The spikes stopped as the shoulder dipped, and the spikes continued up the neck, stopping where the horns were.

After the outline was complete, she began to add in the details of the dragon. She etched in the muscles on her shoulders and legs, adding in the aged lines around her face. She added the large scales under her neck and belly, and focused on the scales that surrounded the rest of her body. Her final touch was adding the lumps and bumps around her face and legs.

When Ember finished her drawing, she took a step back to view it and was quite happy with how it turned out. She had lost track of time while working on it and had not noticed that Jack and Dalka were already done with their task and talking by the fire. When she looked up to survey her work, Dalka called out to her.

"Are you done with your doodle, little one?" asked Dalka as she stood to look at Ember's finished project.

"Yeah," said Ember blushing slightly as the dragon came over to look.

"Oh Ember, it is beautiful." The turquoise dragon breathed. "You did so good, it is quite accurate."

Ember looked down and blushed. She was never complimented very often and she didn't know whether to take it or deny it. She chose to take it, commonly hearing that others preferred that.

"Aw, thank you Dalka," she said touching her friends muzzle gently. "It just gave me something to do to keep my mind off of everything that has happened."

Dalka withdrew her muzzle and cast a glance at Jack who came over to sit next to Ember.

"You know that we are all very proud of you," said Jack. "You have been through more than most adults will ever go through in their lifetime. I am worried about you Ember. I want to make sure that you are okay."

Ember sighed and put down the stick that she had been holding. "I mean physically I am fine, but mentally I am just tired. I am scared, tired and I feel guilty."

"Those are all normal feelings," said Dalka. Ember could hear the hesitation in her voice as if she was not sure how to talk to the girl. "But they will fade over time. None of this is any of our fault, and don't worry too much about it; just take it a day at a time."

Ember sighed and nodded.

"You are a strong girl," Jack told Ember gently as he patted her shoulder. "I don't think that there is a thing in this world you cannot do."

Ember smiled at the man. She realized that he was the picture of what her father used to be. Jack was loving, kind, and supportive. When he made a mistake, he acknowledged it. He gave her and the dragons a home when they had none. He risked his life for her and she was eternally grateful.

She turned and gave the man a hug, burying herself into his embrace. It seemed to surprise him, but he did not miss a beat returning the affection.

"Thank you for everything, Jack," she said, her voice muffled by his clothing.

"Of course." he said gently.

When they parted, they heard the breaking of tree branches and turned to see Cadell come in through the clearing with another deer hanging in his jaws. He dropped it again by the fire and let Jack take it from there.

"Whatever you do not eat we will finish," Cadell said as he lumbered to the other side of the clearing to rest. "Dalka, it is best that we both sleep and rest to regain our strength. We will both eat what is left over of the deer and then take off when night falls."

Ember could see Dalka's eyes narrow. She clearly didn't like being told what to do by the other dragon. Ember thought maybe it made her feel as if she had lost some of her purpose. The turquoise dragon, however, relented, knowing that her friend was right.

Ember watched as Dalka settled herself down on the ground next to Cadell and got comfortable. Ember saw that Jack had already begun preparing the meat and found herself without anything to do again. So, she turned to Jack and tried her best to strike up conversation again.

"Do you think Martha would have come along with us?" Ember asked as Jack continued to work on the deer.

Without looking up Jack laughed. His mood visibly brighter when Ember mentioned his wife. "Oh, yes," Jack chuckled. "There is no doubt in my mind. She would have adored you and Cadell."

"You think so?"

"Absolutely. Martha loved nothing more than a good adventure. I could never get her to sit still!" Jack continued. "I think she would have been happy to see Dalka again. She always loved Dalka just as much as she loved Zimmeran."

"Did she ever fly on Dalka?" Ember asked, hoping to discover whether her suspicions of Jack riding the dragon were true or not.

"Oh yes. We both did. But it was mostly Martha. When Dalka and Zimmeran would come, Dalka would take her out every night for a flight and they would be gone for hours. I liked to fly, but never as much as Martha did. I sometimes would have to pull her off Dalka. She was like a child on a rollercoaster," mused Jack.

Ember smiled, happy that she could help recall memories that Jack was pleased to remember. He handed Ember a piece of cooked meat. They smiled at each other as Jack cooked another. As Ember ate the meat to gain her strength, she looked around the clearing.

I don't want to lose this, she thought to herself. *These are some of the only people in my life who really care for me.* Ember closed her eyes for a moment and she drew in a sharp breath. *I can't lose this.*

13

Ember was pushed into wakefulness by a warm hand ruffling her hair. She hadn't realized that she had fallen asleep after she had eaten her meal.

"Ready to go, kiddo?" Jack asked, smiling.

"Sure," said Ember. She yawned and stretched, feeling Dalka shift from beside her. She guessed the dragon had sat down beside her when she rested. It was odd she didn't wake up with the movement. She stood and tried her best to rub the blur from her eyes. Cadell was waiting for her to come over. She trudged to the awaiting dragon, knowing full well that a whole night of flying lay ahead of them.

Cadell bent down without a word and Ember climbed up on his back. She tried her best to shift into a position that was comfortable for both her and her dragon friend. He rose up and waited for Jack to get upon Dalka. As they waited, Ember looked around. She saw that the fire had been extinguished and the sky was almost black. A light pink adorned the skyline, showing that it was just the beginning of night.

"Where are we going?" Ember asked her black and red partner.

"We are trying to get as close to the island as we possibly can. We don't want to go there yet, we want to work on your powers, see if we can figure them out. See if I can figure out mine too," Cadell admitted. Ember could tell he was reluctant to show weakness. "It is a place your kind calls 'Florida'."

"I know where that is," Ember told the dragon.

"We have another human who will help us. He crafted the crown that our queen is wearing. He has harbored many dragons before us," Dalka called. "Are we ready?"

Ember nodded and got into position, remembering to keep her feet higher up. Jack also got into position.

"Let's do this," said Cadell.

He lunged in the air and Ember stayed low and held on tight, gripping the spikes in front of her and pressing her thighs tightly against Cadell. She could feel each of his strong muscles flex beneath her, working hard to push with his legs. With each beat of his wings, they climbed higher and went faster. They finally leveled out, but continued their speed instead of slowing down. Dalka appeared alongside Cadell, and Jack flashed Ember a smile. A genuine smile. She could tell he really enjoyed flying about as much as she did.

The group pushed on through the night. Sometimes she would look below and see cities. Millions of lights would flash beneath them while cars would rush on interstates. Ember looked up and saw the thousands of stars, untainted by lights. The air was crisp and new as the dragons flew by the dim lights the stars gave.

Cadell's markings glowed dimly as they flew. It made Ember wonder why his markings did that. She reached to touch a marking that was close to her hand to see if it radiated any heat. She touched it, surprised that she felt nothing. She ran her fingers over it, trying to find the source of the light, but to no avail.

"What are you doing?" Cadell called back to her.

"Trying to figure out why your markings are glowing," Ember stated, not taking her hands away from the glowing patch of scales.

The dragon let out a small laugh that shook Ember slightly. "They have been glowing every time we have flown since we left Jack's."

"Do you know why they do that?" she asked curiously.

"No, I don't. That is something I will need to figure out. I do, however, feel stronger every time, so I wonder if it has something to do with my strength."

As they passed over bodies of water, Ember would look down and see their reflections. Cadell would sometimes get close to the water so Ember could put her hand in it as they flew past. It sprayed around them and lit up a light blue with her touch. Cadell's wing dipped and he too sprayed the water around them.

The dragons began to descend from the clouds hours after they had departed from the clearing. The air smelled salty and felt humid. They landed in the middle of the woods where a nice house sat alone with a small barn. It was completely different from Jack's house. The place seemed nicely kept with a neat garden, newly mowed lawn, and a freshly painted barn. Dogs began to bark in kennels by the red barn before lights turned on in the house.

"Who's there?" a man's voice called out. "I have a gun and am not afraid to shoot!"

"That would be a fatal mistake," Cadell called beneath Ember. His voice was low in warning, and she knew that he was not playing.

The porch light flicked on revealing a man in a robe holding a shotgun pointed at the two dragons and humans.

When he saw the dragons, he lowered the gun. His mouth opened in shock and then it turned into a smile.

"What are you doing here?" he asked, leaning the weapon against the side of the house and jumping down the porch stairs. "Jane! Come out here!"

A woman came out and looked at the dragons and unlike the man seemed a bit troubled with their arrival. Cadell puffed smoke out of his nostrils as the lady looked at them.

"The female does not seem very thrilled," Cadell snarled. "Should we fix that?"

Ember put her hand on her friend's shoulder as Dalka growled at Cadell in warning.

"I am sorry for the unexpected visit. This was the only safe place I could think of that was near our home. I know you have harbored our kind before. I was hoping you could help us again."

The man nodded his head. "Of course. Anything to help Amrendra," he said, walking over to them.

When Ember and Jack got down on the ground, they walked over to the man who had his hand stretched out. The woman stayed back on the porch, looking at them with large frightened eyes. She seemed hesitant and unsure how to handle herself in the overwhelming situation.

"I am Drake and the lady by the door is Jane. Forgive her, she is just tired. She always gets stressed when we house

you guys, but she will loosen up," Drake said, shaking both
Jack's and Ember's hands. He looked up at the dragons. "It
is an honor that you chose me to help you. Is there anything
I can do to make things easier? The barn is all yours; I will
put straw and hay in there and put out some water troughs.
Your two companions can sleep in the house. I will give
them everything they need."

Ember looked at the man timidly. "If it is okay with
you, I would like to sleep out in the barn with my friends."

Drake smiled warmly, "Yes of course. I will bring out
some blankets, pillows, and a heater."

He began walking to the barn. "Although come along
and change! Jane, can you make these people something to
eat? And run a bath for them? Get the guest bedroom set
up for the gentleman and some blankets out for the girl!"

Jane nodded and helped Jack and Ember inside. It
was a nice, cozy modern home the couple had. A grey cat
meowed as they entered, rubbing up against Ember's legs.
She bent down to scratch its head as it purred. Jane was
busily running in and out of rooms, starting water and
gathering clothes and blankets. She gently grabbed Ember's
hand and led her to a small bathroom where a tub was
steaming ready for her.

Jane turned to leave before hesitating.

"Are you that missing girl from Montana?" she asked.

"Yes," Ember replied, not meeting her eyes.

"They didn't force you to go, did they? They didn't do
anything to you? Do you need help? I won't tell anyone, I
promise," Jane asked.

Ember almost laughed, but she held it back and smiled
at the concerned woman.

"No, it was my decision to come along with them. Originally it was just me and the dragons, but Jack ended up coming along with us after PFIB barged onto his land," she explained.

"I didn't even know the dragons existed until they all started coming and Drake had to explain everything to me. I thought they were just legends," Jane said. "It must have been so overwhelming for you. I know it was for me."

"I thought they were too," replied Ember. "And yeah, it was a bit nerve-racking at first, especially meeting Cadell," Ember mused. "I shot him the first time we met because he was on my property and I thought he was going to kill me. But it doesn't do anything because their scales are bullet-proof. After I got to know the dragons, and learn about them, I now trust them completely. Cadell comes off a bit rough around the edges, but really, he is amazing."

Jane nodded and smiled, closing the door softly behind her. Ember stripped her clothes. When something fell loudly to the floor, she realized it was her phone.

Oh, wow. She thought. *I didn't think that it would have stayed in my pocket. I didn't even remember it! It is probably dead by now.*

Just as Ember suspected, it was. She put it on the counter and slipped into the warm bath. She cleaned herself, scrubbing her wind-tangled hair the best she could. When the water was no longer warm, she got out and dried herself off, putting on the new clothes.

She walked out and could see Jack washed and changed, eating soup at the kitchen table. Jane had created a pile of pillows and blankets, and like Drake had said, a heater was next to it. Ember glanced at the clock on the stove, it read

4:30. Ember was shocked it was so early in the morning, but her stomach grumbled, pulling her attention to the hot bowl of soup on the table.

She sat down next to Jack eating the soup hungrily, not realizing that she had needed the food.

"I told you that they would figure everything out," said Jack after he had finished, wiping his grey beard with a napkin.

"Yeah. I didn't know that they had this many ties," Ember said. She didn't really like it, but she was too hungry to care.

"Me neither," admitted Jack. "However, I have learned to not doubt anything."

When Ember had finished, Drake had come in and began to carry everything out to the barn. When he came back to grab the heater, he told Ember to follow him.

"How do you know the dragons?" asked Ember. Dalka had not told her how they knew Drake, and Ember wondered if his story was as epic as her own.

"Well, a dragon who was searching for another landed in these woods. It's a long flight from their island to here," said Drake. "They told me they had lost a hatchling and had stopped to rest when I found them. My family lived in this house, and my parents decided to help the dragons. So ever since, our house kind of became a dragon pit stop," he laughed. "They helped my family thrive, and repaid us with jewels and gems. The queen even came and thanked me. That was recently and she explained everything that was happening and asked if I knew anything, which I did not. She did talk about the prophecy. It was really amazing. I took some of the gems and crafted her a crown, and I just kinda became friends with the dragons ever since," Drake shrugged.

Ember nodded. "Well, thank you for helping them."

Drake smiled. "Of course. I am guessing you are Ember Winters?"

"In the flesh," said Ember repaying the smile.

"I have heard a lot about you," said Jake, his smile growing sad. "Thank you, thank you for your sacrifice."

Ember's smile turned into a forced one as her stomach dropped. Although the prophecy did not state it was her, everyone, even this stranger, seemed to think it was. She always forgot about that part of the prophecy, and it tended to slip her mind often. She tried her best not to think about it.

"Yeah, of course," she said.

They opened the barn door and saw the two dragons sitting comfortably in the middle of the barn on a nice pile of hay. There were quite a few water troughs filled to the brim with fresh water. A gentle light was cast from a single antler chandelier held in the middle top of the barn. Some cats meowed from above in a hayloft and a cow lazily chewed its cud in a small stall, seemingly unfazed by the large creatures sharing its space.

"Welcome," Dalka said, peering down at the humans. "We sincerely thank you, Drake, for taking us in. I will be sure to repay you."

Drake laughed. "It is no problem at all, and I told you guys there is no need to repay me." He looked around the barn as if to check everything over before turning to leave. "If you guys need anything, just come in the house at any time. Stay as long as you need." Drake turned and closed the barn door softly behind him, leaving the three to themselves.

"Do you feel better?" asked Dalka as Ember began to set up a place to sleep.

"Yeah, I am just tired," she replied.

"Why did you choose to sleep with us?" Cadell questioned coming over to the girl.

"I don't know. I can go inside if you want. But I just wanted to be with you guys," she said as she plugged in the heater.

"Do what you wish," Cadell said settling in beside the makeshift bed she made. "It makes it easier to keep watch over you and make sure you don't do anything stupid."

Ember glared at the dragon and yawned, climbing underneath the blanket and angling the heater so it would blow the warm air on her. Warm and comfortable, she began to drift off to sleep as two large heads came to rest on either side of her

· · · · ·

Ember awoke to the sun shining in her face and the dragons talking to each other again. A few barn cats had curled up around her and she scratched their heads gently.

"Good to see you awake, small one," Dalka said turning her attention to Ember. "We must get started working on your powers again as soon as possible. Go inside and eat, return when you are done."

Ember pushed herself up and went into the house where she saw pancakes on the table and the three adults eating them.

"Good morning! Pancakes are ready!" said Jane motioning with her fork for her to sit down.

"Thank you!" said Ember smiling as she set down at the old oak table.

Jack smiled at the girl as she sat down.

"I have explained to these fine people everything that has happened and now we need to come up with a plan," said Jack, setting down his fork.

Ember who had just started eating, finished chewing before swallowing.

"The chances of PFIB finding you here are slim," said Drake. "However, I want to take all the precautions just in case something was to happen. We have dealt with them before. So, we have a few ideas on how to avoid them."

"What would those be?" asked Ember nervously.

"Just general things. We need to make your presence outside of our house and barn very limited. We will take you to the city a couple of times to get the things you need in the right size. But the main thing is making sure strangers or friends that come to visit do not see you. All I ask is when you see someone come to our house, just hide in the barn."

"What happens if PFIB does find us?" asked Ember.

"To be honest we pray or we try our best to escape on the back of the dragons," Jack said. "You saw how hard it was for us to escape last time, you almost got killed in the process. It is so important that we do not get caught. I would be killed almost immediately, but you and the dragons would be caught and tortured for information."

"Well, that is soothing," Ember muttered.

"Then let's do what we can to avoid getting caught," said Jane. "When we go out to the city, we will conceal your identity so you are not seen or discovered."

Ember and Jack nodded in understanding as they continued to eat the pancakes.

"Is there a time that you would like to go the city?" Jane asked looking at Ember.

Ember shook her head and swallowed. "No, I am fine with whatever time is best for you."

Jane smiled at the girl's courtesy but did not say more.

She scarfed down the buttermilk pancakes quickly and thanked Jane for the meal before heading back outside to the barn. She walked in and she saw that both dragons were in the same position she had left them.

They turned their heads to see her enter and lowered themselves in order to be eye level.

"We will most likely be going to the city sometime today, so I don't want you to worry when we leave," Ember said as she sat in a rocking chair by the window.

Dalka huffed and shuffled with concern. "I don't know if that is such a good idea. Can't they just go without you?"

"We will be fine. We are hiding our identity," Ember explained. "And plus, I think that I will go crazy if I don't go. I feel like it has been forever since I have been out."

Dalka did not say anything, but the look on Cadell's face spoke volumes for both dragons. His brow was creased in a worried scowl and his eyes were hard as he looked out the window, not meeting Ember's eyes.

"Don't worry guys, I will come back."

"If you don't, I will kill whoever hurt you three times over," Cadell growled.

She knew that was as close as she was going to get to consent. She smiled and laughed.

"Alright, I promise I will come back, and you have

permission to kill whomever prevented me from doing so as many times as you want."

They ceased talk of that conversation and Ember sat in silence, reflecting on what was happening.

When her mind fluttered over to her powers, she looked up at the dragons. They noticed her concentrated expression as she looked at them and it was Dalka who decided to speak.

"What are you thinking, small one?" Dalka asked cocking her head to the side.

"If I have the power to create Merocomee stones, what else do I have the power to do?" Ember asked.

"Ember, we have been over this. I told you that I don't kn—"

"I know that you don't. But I meant that as a rhetorical question, but also I wanted us all to think about it." Ember stopped and closed her eyes.

"Ever since that time in the clearing when I felt all that anger, I have now been able to feel this power in my core. If I concentrate hard enough, I can bring it to my fingertips. But what if there is nothing there for it to turn to Merocomee?"

Ember stopped for a moment and closed her eyes, concentrating on the power she felt in her core. At first, she worried because she felt nothing, but she could then feel it rise. She was able to get it to rise high enough to gain control and she then worked it down to her fingertips. The whole process took about seven minutes, which made Ember worry about how slow it was. She opened her eyes and looked at the dragons when she felt the energy and power pool around her fingertips.

"Okay. I have it. But I am worried it took me that long," she said.

"I would most likely guess that it will get faster as time goes on. When you get better it will become second nature. Remember in the clearing it only took seconds?" Dalka said.

"You're right!" Ember said. She returned her attention back to the energy she had called out. "Well, nothing seems to be happening with my fingertips."

"Touch something," Cadell said. He leaned forward and Ember could tell he was just as eager as she was to see what would happen.

Ember touched the arm of the chair that she was sitting in, full expecting something to happen. When nothing did, she lifted her hand up, disappointed.

"Well, that didn't work," she sighed.

She then lifted her gaze to the dragons again. Dalka seemed to get her notion and bent her head down for the girl to touch. Ember put her fingertips to the dragon's nose and the dragon closed her eyes. Ember's fingertips began to glow and she felt some of her energy transferring over to Dalka.

The dragon immediately jerked her head away in confusion. "I felt like I was being healed!" Dalka exclaimed.

"It would make sense. My markings glow and I always feel stronger when I am around her. See?" Cadell explained, while making his markings glow. "But I wonder if I am also able to give energy to her," Cadell said. "I know that I don't have the powers that you do. But I am able to channel my energy. I think I can reverse the flow and give you back energy, but I also believe we can both take it from each other."

Cadell bent his head and pushed his nose to the girl's arm. Ember felt his energy pour into her. It was warm and smooth, making her feel relaxed and at peace.

She pulled away before he could give her anymore energy.

"Whoa! That was an odd feeling!"

"Now, let me see if the other part is true," Cadell said. "Ember, I will not take much."

He stepped back and Ember felt her energy suddenly drain. It was gradual, but she definitely felt something sapping her energy. She looked over and saw Cadell's markings beginning to glow. He stopped and he sighed.

"Yes, it's true. It can go both ways. See if you can block me, Ember," Cadell instructed.

Ember focused and retreated her energy back to her core, constructing a mental wall to keep Cadell away. She did not feel her energy drain, but felt Cadell trying to get inside.

When it didn't work, he relented. "Very good, Ember. I am impressed," Cadell said. "It is crucial for you to be able to do that. Even though I am the only one that can take your energy, I could lose my cool by accident and drain some, so it is important you know how to deter me if need be. However, I do not know if it works on other creatures."

"It worked on me," Ember suggested.

"Yes, but you are part of the prophecy," Dalka contradicted. "No other human has the ability to focus energy like you do; it is divine intervention. And neither does any dragon besides Cadell. To be honest, I do not know how you got the powers. That is beyond any living creature's ability to really comprehend. All we can do is trust that everything will work out."

Ember moved over to a cat that had curled up next to her chair. She pushed the energy back to her fingertips again and touched the feline.

The cat raised its head at the touch and rubbed against Ember's hand. It didn't seem to be fazed. She then tried a new route and tried to draw energy. She retreated her energy back and tried her best to suck in energy.

She began to feel energy pouring into her and she looked up.

"I think I am drawing energy from the cat!"

"No, you're drawing it from me," said Cadell from behind her.

She immediately stopped and laughed. "Sorry, Cadell!"

He only huffed and turned.

"Well, I suppose you can only give energy to other dragons and take from one another," Dalka concluded.

"It seems reasonable," Ember said.

"There is, however, much more to discover," said Dalka. "We are only scratching the surface of what you are capable of. With your determination and Cadell's power, I really don't think there isn't anything you can't do."

CHAPTER

14

Ember was very eager to get out and into the city. Jane had thrown hats and glasses onto Jack and Ember in order to conceal their identity. Ember sat in the back of an old blue pickup truck as Drake drove down the highway heading to a small city. She watched as other cars passed by her. She found it odd she missed something as simple as riding in a car as much as she did. They pulled into a mall and all four of the new acquaintances got out of the truck, slamming doors behind them.

"Ok, let's meet back at the truck by 4:30," said Drake. "If something happens, just call me. Stick together. I don't want anything happening to you girls."

Both groups split off, Jane went with Ember and Drake with Jack. They first headed into a makeup store and Ember scrunched her nose in disgust.

"You are welcome to choose whatever," Jane said smiling and looking at Ember. When she noticed her more displeased look, her face changed to a more amused expression. "You don't like makeup, do you?" she laughed.

"No, not really. I always found it too much work. And why put that stuff on your face? I am happy with the way

I am." Ember stated turning on her heel and walking out of the store.

"I like that about you," Jane said. "I wish when I was your age that I had that sort of self-confidence."

"It isn't self-confidence," Ember sighed as she walked. "If it was, I would think I was beautiful. I am happy with the way I am because I follow one simple philosophy; I never fight for what I cannot win. Like those pretty schoolgirls chasing a boy like a house dog chases a rabbit. It isn't much use. If you know you can't get something, give up. I know that makeup won't make me any prettier, so I work on what I have on the inside."

"I don't know if I would go with that philosophy. Why stop? You never know what you might accomplish," Jane said, weary of the teen's way of thinking.

"That is where belief comes into play. Confidence and belief are often confused. If you believe in something, you have complete faith in it. But if you're confident, you can easily retreat back. You don't fully stand by what you're confident in. If you tell someone that you are confident a horse will win in a race and it loses, they don't look on you as poorly as if you said you believed it would win. If I go for something, I believe in it. I believe I will get something if I put my time and effort into it. If I don't, I learn and move forward. But I go into it having faith." Ember said.

Jane smiled as the pair entered a clothing store. The AC hit them as she looked at the girl beside her. "I think I like that part much better."

"Most people do," Ember shrugged. "But the vast majority don't ask any questions past the first part. It's only those who ask me who get to hear the full thing."

They spent a half an hour sifting through clothes and calling on one another if they found something. They got together a small bundle that Ember liked and Jane bought the girl the clothes. As they were leaving, Ember looked up at Jane.

"What can I do to repay you? It doesn't feel right for you to be buying me all of these clothes."

"Consider it from the dragons," Jane said. "We are quite comfortable with all the jewels the dragons give us as a thank you to our services."

That made Ember smile and feel better.

"Drake and I don't spend a lot of money on ourselves. We spend it mostly on others," Jane explained. "It has never been in our nature to often splurge on ourselves."

Ember nodded her head in understanding, smiling at the kindness that Drake and Jane radiated off of them.

They continued through the mall, stopping at stores that either Ember or Jane found interesting. When the time came that they needed to meet up by the truck, they found that Jack and Drake were not there. After waiting a half an hour, they never came. Jane tried to call Drake's cell phone, but it had been turned off or died.

"What do you think happened to them?" asked Ember, worry etched clearly on her face.

"I honestly don't know," said Jane putting the keys into the ignition of the old truck. "Knowing Drake, he got caught up in some store he found, but it is unlike him to have his phone turned off."

The truck sputtered and then roared to life with some prompting from Jane. She shifted gears and flashed a look at Ember. "Let's go find them."

She drove through the parking lot of the mall and Ember looked around, trying her best to spot the two men. They kept on driving in circles, but they could not spot them. Jane continued to try and call her husband, but to no avail.

As the sky began to turn dark, both the teen and the woman realized that they had a problem. They could not call the police, as they would surely search the barn and find traces of the dragons, and they would find Ember and return her home. The only solution was they would have to find the two missing people themselves. Jane pulled onto the highway and sped back to their place of refuge as fast as the truck could go. She narrowly avoided police officers as she sped, but both made it back to the small home without incident.

As soon as the truck came to a halt, Ember jumped out of the passenger side and ran to the barn, desperate to ask Dalka and Cadell for help.

"Cadell! Dalka!" She cried out, pushing the barn doors open.

Both dragons were already on their feet, snarling as the girl burst through the door. Cadell's markings had bathed the whole barn in a dark, blood red light. She could only see the shadowy figures of the dragons lit up by the light of Cadell.

"Drake and Jack are missing. I don't know where they are. They went into the mall and then they never met us," Ember explained.

"I knew that going out would be a bad idea," snarled Dalka. Her tail lashed, hitting a support beam. It made the whole barn shake for a moment before Cadell spoke up.

"We will find them. You and Jane stay back," Cadell said.

"No!" Ember hollered, putting her hands out to block the entrance. She knew that it wouldn't stop the large creatures from going out if their heart was set on it, but she hoped that her presence by the door would at least deter them somewhat.

"I have an idea. But I don't know if it will work," Ember said.

She walked over quickly to a water trough and stuck her hand inside, again feeling the odd warm tingly sensation go up her arm. The water trough began to glow, giving them enough light to see the image it created inside.

Jack and Drake were sitting in the back of a van, gagged and tied with ropes. Ember gasped and she called out to Jane.

"Jane! Jane! Come in here quick! We found them!" Ember called.

It only took a couple seconds before Jane burst through the barn. Out of breath and exasperated, she held onto the side of the door, panting. "Where are they?"

"I don't know exactly where, but I know what happened to them," Ember said, motioning for Jane to come and look into the water trough.

When Jane peered over, her hand flew up to her mouth in shock. Ember could clearly see that she was upset, but Ember could not join in her distress. She knew that there was a job for her to do, and she understood she was the only one able to do it.

"We just need to find the location." Ember said. She eyed the trough in hope that it would give her an answer.

It did. The image zoomed out to reveal that the vehicle they were in was parked in a place called Liberty Plaza.

It looked like a normal office building, but Ember had to guess that it wasn't normal inside at all.

Her main question was who had taken them? And why?

Ember guessed it was PFIB, but she could not know for certain. Jane, seeing the opportunity, quickly put the name into her phone and got directions from the barn. It was about an hour drive, but she knew with the dragons they would be there in about fifteen minutes.

Both the dragons, Ember, and Jane exited the barn and Ember got on the back of Cadell, eager to go and get her friends back.

She saw Jane looking worried and a bit out of place by the barn door.

"Jane?" Dalka called from beside Ember. "Do you want to come with me?"

Ember looked at Dalka with the look a child would give when a mother allowed a sibling to come along. Ember was frustrated, she saw how distraught Jane was at that moment. She knew that if she continued to be that way, she would drag them down and they would not be able to properly think and execute a plan. In order to save Jack and Drake, they would need to be level-headed and calm.

Dalka tossed Ember a short look, a silent command to keep her mouth shut and obey the dragon. Ember bit her tongue, swallowing the urge to argue. She waited as patiently as she could for Dalka to explain how to fly to Jane, and they then took flight.

Cadell flew farther ahead of Dalka and Jane and called back to Ember.

"I don't think Dalka should have invited Jane to come along," Cadell told Ember. "If she dies, that's on Dalka."

"I agree," Ember said. "We need to be approaching this calmly. We can't afford to have her panic give us away."

Cadell stayed silent and continued to fly. After a moment or two, he spoke again. This time he changed the topic and tone of his voice. "Ember?" Cadell asked.

Ember looked at her friend, concerned at the severity in his voice. "Yeah?"

"If Dalka or I tell you to do something, do it," Cadell said.

Ember's worry changed to clear agitation as she crossed her arms. "Just because you guys are older than me doesn't mean you get to boss me around and act like I am a child. I have been through my fair share of things. I am more mature than most adults."

"I have no doubt of that," Cadell growled. "At the end of the day, you are only seventeen, Ember. Dalka and I have been through the ringer a time or two, trust me. I wouldn't ask you to do something I didn't think you needed to do, and I know Dalka wouldn't either."

Ember huffed, but she didn't say a word. She knew that she was outmatched.

Cadell banked and Ember looked behind her to see that Dalka had also turned. She remembered that Jane had her phone and was directing Dalka on where to go. She looked below and saw that they were circling a building, and Ember called out to Cadell.

"We need to find a place to land so we can figure out what to do," Ember shouted over the wind.

Cadell did not say anything, but she knew he had heard her when they began to descend.

Dalka followed suit as they found a small patch of

woods big enough to conceal the dragons and their human companions. The dragons landed and allowed Jane and Ember to get off.

"Do you think it would just be best to tear the building down?" Ember asked.

"No, we would risk killing Jack and Drake," Dalka contradicted.

"We don't even know where they are now. It could be as simple as just breaking into the van if they are still in it," Jane added.

"I need water," Ember said.

"You know, you could have gotten a drink before we left," spat Cadell. "Because I am not waltzing up to a vender to buy you a drink. I mean, I don't even have any money! So, what do I do? Just rip off one of my scales and say 'Oh, I am a dragon, so I don't have any money. Please accept one of my scales.' Yeah Ember, we can totally do that and not cause a scene. Go drink out of a puddle."

"You know, for being the chosen one you're not the brightest crayon in the box," Jane said, covering her mouth trying not to laugh.

"What the hell is a crayon?"

"My point exactly," Jane concluded.

Dalka sighed, clearly also amused by her friend's lack of understanding. "What Ember means is she needs a place to work her powers."

When the realization hit Cadell of what he had done, his marking glowed brightly and Ember was trying her best not to lose it.

"I knew that!" Cadell grumbled defensively, lashing his tail. He puffed out smoke as he tried his best to conceal his embarrassment, but the trio saw right past it and allowed the dragon to escape with his pride.

"Sure, you did," snickered Ember. "But going into a store isn't a bad idea. It's dry all around, so there are no puddles or ponds. I, however, do not have any cash on me."

Jane smiled and she stuck her hand in her pocket, bringing out a stack of twenty-dollar bills. "I never leave the house without cash. Best habit I have ever got myself into."

Ember smiled and she breathed a sigh of relief.

Maybe bringing Jane was not a bad idea after all.

"You both stay here," Ember told the dragons. "We will be back as soon as we can."

"Are you sure you will be okay?" Cadell asked. He sounded angry, but Ember knew that was his way of covering up his anxiety.

"Yes, Cadell, I promise that we will be fine. We will holler if something happens."

The dragon bent his head down and touched the girl's cheek. "Alright."

Jane and Ember walked for a couple of minutes before they found themselves dumped onto a deserted sidewalk. They looked across the street and found a small dollar store and Ember looked over at Jane.

"Well, isn't that convenient?" Ember laughed.

"Sure is," commented Jane as they both crossed the street. "That's why they call it a convenience store."

When they entered, the smell of cleaner and cardboard struck Ember's nose harshly and she scrunched it up to try and lessen the smell. A man who looked to be in his fifties looked up from a book he was reading to peer at them before returning to it without a word. Ember did not like the vibe the place gave off, but she knew that she had no other choice but to proceed if she wanted to save the two men.

"I will find water, you find a bowl," Ember told Jane.

Jane nodded and departed to find the items. Ember began looking through the shelves to find a bowl, but before she could find one, she heard the automatic doors open. She looked up, only expecting it to be just another person looking for something they needed late at night. But instead she saw two men walk in with the acronym PFIB in bold letters on their shirts.

They looked nothing like the agents who had caught her in the barn. These agents were wearing suits instead of the armored uniforms and vests Ember had seen the other agents sporting. She immediately looked around for something to conceal her identity. She found herself near a party department. She threw on a pair of large sunglasses and put her hair in a bun and threw on a party hat and scarf. She knew she looked ridiculous, but it served the purpose.

"Why hello there, Miss! We just need to squeeze past you! We are having a Christmas party and need to get some plates," the voice said, sounding deep and kind.

Ember moved and her heart caught in her throat as she saw the suits of the PFIB men slide past her. She turned around and walked away, focused on getting out alive.

She almost made it out of the aisle before she heard Jane call from the other side of the store.

"Ember! I found some water!" She yelled.

Well can you make it any more obvious? Ember thought bitterly as she froze in her tracks.

She could feel the stares of the men on her back and heard footsteps from behind and she broke out into a run. On the way, she found a pack of plastic cups and grabbed them, knowing that it was better than nothing.

"Jane, let's go!" Ember shouted as she passed the item detector. It blared loudly and she pushed her legs faster as she crossed the street. She saw a car fast approaching as she and Jane both stepped onto the street and she heard the squealing of tires. Ember didn't comprehend anything until she was shoved out of the way by Jane and she fell hard onto the pavement.

She heard a loud smack behind her and turned just in time to see both PFIB officials run the opposite direction. She saw Jane in a pool of blood, squirming and moaning in pain.

Ember realized what had happened and yelled for her friends.

"Dalka! Cadell! Help us, please!" Ember cried out.

"Oh my gosh! I am so sorry! I am calling 911 now! But you guys just walked right out in front of me!" said a frantic teenage girl who looked to be Ember's age. She had a cell phone in her hand and was getting ready to dial 911 before Ember stood up to face her.

Ember was calm, but deadly serious. "If you know what's best for you, get into the car, do not call 911, and don't breathe a word of what you see."

The girl nodded and it was in that moment Ember realized she still had the disguise on she had stolen from the dollar store and realized she must look incredibly crazy. She heard trees breaking and crashing as the dragon tore through to reach the girl and the woman.

"What happened?" said Cadell, markings glaring dangerously bright as he prepared himself for battle.

"Jane got hit by a car. Don't hurt the driver; it was our
fault. We ran in front of her. We got water and cups. We
just need to get back to the clearing and help Jane."

Cadell didn't waste any time and he picked up both
Jane and Ember in his talons just as Dalka broke through
the trees. She didn't have time to survey the scene, but she
followed her friend back to the clearing.

Cadell landed on his rear legs before putting Ember
down and setting Jane gently down beside her.

"Jane! Are you alright?" Ember asked frantically.

The woman moaned and stirred. "Yeah, she just got
my leg."

"What the hell happened?" Dalka asked angrily.

"There is nothing we can do," Cadell said. "It was their
mistake, not the person who hit Jane."

"What?" Dalka said confused.

The air around them was frantic and Ember knew an
explanation was going to be the only way to calm it.

"We went into a store and some PFIB officials started
to chase us, so we ran. I didn't look because I was more
concerned about getting caught and we crossed the street.
Jane pushed me out of the way when a car almost hit me,"
Ember explained. Her voice softened. "I am so sorry Jane.
This is all my fault."

"No, it is not," Jane said sternly. Ember saw Jane throw
something and it landed at her feet. She realized that it was
a bottle of water. "Now do your magic thingy and go and
save my husband."

"What about you?" asked Ember.

"I'll be fine. I can wait until all of this is over," Jane said.

"I will stay with her," Dalka said sitting beside the injured women. "Just do what you need to do and be quick, Ember."

"Alright," said Ember picking up the bottle of water. She took off the party disguise and threw it on the ground.

She ripped open the pack of plastic cups and poured the water into one and stuck a couple fingers inside. The image that appeared was not as strong as the one she had seen in the trough. Ember guessed it had to do with the amount of skin she put into the water. The more skin, the clearer the image. However, the small fuzzy image was enough to get them by.

Ember could see that both Jack and Drake were in the same place they had last seen them. Cadell was peering in from behind Ember, trying to get a good look at the image as well.

"It seems like they are still in the van," Ember concluded. "We are too far. Can you fly me over there, Cadell?"

The dragon did not reply, but he bent down and Ember got on him. When he stood, Ember realized she had no idea which direction the van was. When she tried to say something, Cadell lunged into the air catching her off.

He pushed air beneath them both with his powerful wings, surging into the night sky with intention. They only leveled out for a brief second before Cadell began to descend. He banked, clearly trying to find a place to land without being seen. Dismayed, Ember saw that there was no way they could stay hidden.

"We are just going to have to land next to the vehicle and proceed with as much haste as we can muster," Cadell said.

"Sounds like a plan," Ember agreed, bracing herself as Cadell began his rapid descent.

Before they could reach the ground, alarms began to wail around them and hundreds of soldiers began to pour from the office building. They were all armed with guns and began to shoot at the dragon and the girl.

Letting out a startled roar, Cadell tried to land as the bullets pelted him. He fell harshly and Ember was sent flying onto the pavement. She landed on her back hard. It knocked the wind out her and she groaned in pain.

"Ember!" she heard the dragon roar from behind her.

She looked and saw he had already gotten to his feet. She saw him jump at her and she shielded herself and covered her eyes full expecting the weight of the dragon to crush her. When she opened her eyes, she saw that Cadell had covered her with his body and was shielding her from the onslaught of bullets. She heard the clanking of bullets hitting him and she immediately felt sorry for her friend.

"I am giving you one final warning!" She heard her friend bellow from above her. "Cease your fire or else!"

Ember did not hear the bullets slow or stop and she felt her friend tense up. She heard Cadell take a deep breath of air and then felt the heat of the dragon's flame all around her. She knew he had burned everything around him, and she prayed he had left the van unscathed. After a moment, Cadell shifted and allowed Ember to step out from beneath him.

She saw hundreds of dead and burned bodies but did her best to avoid looking at them for too long. It made her stomach churn and she turned her head and vomited, not able to take the stench of burning flesh. She tried her best to push past the feelings of fear and confusion. She now understood why Cadell had tried to protect her. She knew she needed to have a clear head if she was going to save her two friends.

She felt Cadell's muzzle on her back. She knew that it was his way of saying that he was there with her.

"I am sorry, Ember," Cadell said. "You are safe now."

When she was able to see past the watering of her eyes, she spotted the van and quickly made her way over to it. She wiped her nose with her sleeve and stepped over the bodies of the soldiers. Cadell followed close behind her and she could feel the ground shaking as he ran. She opened the back and saw Jack and Drake staring back at her. They were both drenched in sweat and Ember had to guess it was from Cadell's flame. She quickly got Jack untied and he immediately took a breath for air.

"Oh, thank God," Jack breathed. "We were just—"

"Shut up and help me!" Ember shouted as he finished the last of his ropes and moved to Drake.

Together, Jack and Ember freed Drake. They scrambled out of the back of the van. Cadell saw them and bent down to let them on. Ember stopped and let Drake and Jack get in front of her before turning to follow.

Ember felt something grab her leg and she let out a startled scream and fell.

They looked and saw that a PFIB agent had grabbed her leg.

He isn't dead.

"Get off her!" she heard Cadell snarl.

"Help...me." the soldier groaned, his burned hand squeezing her leg.

"I c-can't...I'm...I'm sorry," Ember croaked through the tears.

She shook her leg violently and ran to Cadell, vaulting onto his back, praying that he would just take off and leave everything behind.

She could feel Cadell take off quickly, just as she heard the faint sound of the first emergency vehicles approaching.

"Drake, Jane was hurt and you need to take her to the hospital. Dalka is with her in the clearing, but she insisted we come and rescue you both first," Ember said, not looking behind her.

"Is she alright?" Drake asked.

Ember could tell from the man's tone of voice he was on the verge of panic and she tried her best to reassure him. "Yes, she will be fine. She just hurt her leg. She saved me from getting hit by a car. I owe her my life."

Cadell began to descend back into the clearing where Dalka and Jane both were. Cadell couldn't fully land before Drake had already scrambled off his back to get to his wife and check on her.

"Jane! Jane! Honey, are you ok? Ember told me what happened! Oh, why did you come along?" Drake said frantically checking his wife over.

"Yes, I am fine," Jane laughed. Although her voice was strained with pain, she still had a bright smile on her face and she sounded happy.

"Just hold on, I am calling the ambulance," said Drake taking Jane's phone. "Ember, you, Jack and the dragons go back to the house."

"We can't!" hollered Ember distressed. "They will find us and I cannot have your house destroyed like Jack's."

"That is why we have two houses." Jane spoke up. "We have a house that the government knows about, and a house that only us and a few chosen people know about. We never stay at that house, but all our mail and everything legal is directed there, not to the house where we currently live. There are no ties between the houses; it will be impossible to find. Even though my family used to live in it, we had the house 'destroyed', or so the government thinks. Do not worry, you will all be safe. I have dealt with this before."

Ember studied Drake for a moment before she gave in and got on Cadell. Jack, who had not said a word, got onto Dalka. Before they took off, Ember looked down at the couple.

"Be safe, alright?" Ember called. "I didn't go through all that trouble to save you only for you to get killed."

Drake laughed, but he then turned serious. "Don't worry Ember, I will be safe. And thank you, all of you," he said looking around him. "I owe you my life."

CHAPTER

15

When they returned, both the dragons, Ember and Jack had spent the night in the barn. They were all too restless to sleep and spoke about the events that transpired.

"I figured it was PFIB who took you guys," Ember said as she sat in a pile of hay. "The moment you didn't come out to the truck, I figured something was wrong. Then when Drake didn't answer his phone, I was positive that something had happened."

"Well, it was really odd," Jack said as he nursed a wound on his head with an ice pack. "They came out of nowhere in the store we were in. I mean they were everywhere, Ember. They told us they were the police, so no one in the store even questioned it. There was even a police car that passed the store! They didn't even stop. It goes to show you, Ember, these people can really get what they want. They work above the law."

"This is what makes this whole situation harder and more dangerous," Dalka added. "They are learning. They learned from this trip that bullets won't hurt us, they also learned we breathe fire. They can now come up with new weapons and ways to defend themselves from us.

They can evolve, and it's not just one being. It is thousands of humans. That's what makes them so dangerous."

"Now they know for sure that Drake is affiliated with us, and that makes it even harder for us to get the things we need and travel to the places we have to go," Jack stated. "We have to be more careful."

"Drake said he had dealt with PFIB before, but I do not know what he means by that," Ember said.

"He has helped our kind before, correct, Dalka?" Cadell asked.

The turquoise dragon nodded in affirmation before the black dragon continued.

"It would make sense that they would have had him on their radar. I mean, yes, keeping dragons here would surely hide them from the public eye, but exchanging the stones that other dragons have given him must raise some suspicion."

"Do you believe they traced him back using the stones?" Jack asked.

"I know they captured the both of you because you were there, Jack. Even seemingly covered, it is not possible to completely change your identity in a matter of a few days."

"I know for a fact you're right, Cadell," said Jack. "But I believe it is something we are going to have to talk to Drake about when he returns with Jane."

"I hope Jane is okay," Ember said. She took a stray piece of hay she had found and twirled it around her fingers. "I can't help but feel this is my fault."

"You can only be so careful when you have a pack of gun-wielding agents on your ass," Jack soothed. "Don't beat yourself up over it, kid."

They continued to talk until they heard an engine coming into the driveway. They all held their breath and stayed quiet, remembering the warning that Drake had given them about not coming out if someone came. They stayed still until the engine faded away and Jane and Drake entered the barn.

"Welcome back," Dalka greeted. "Are you well, Jane?"

Ember saw that Dalka had grown to like Jane. Ember had to guess that it was because both the dragon and the woman were similar.

"Yes, I am fine." She smiled. Her leg was completely cast up and she hobbled on a pair of crutches. However, even in her state, Jane continued to smile.

"We were able to get a friend of ours to drop us off. We told a couple white lies, but it all worked out," Drake explained. "Dalka, Cadell, all woods behind the house and barn are yours to hunt in. There is plenty of game, I promise. As for the rest of us, let's go eat breakfast."

Everyone exited the barn and the group of humans went into the house. Drake, now becoming the caregiver since Jane was out of commission, made breakfast. As he cooked, Ember brought up the conversation they had in the barn.

"Hey, Drake?" Ember called.

He hummed in response as he flipped an egg he was frying.

"What do you mean you have dealt with PFIB before?" Ember asked.

"As you know, I have housed dragons," Drake began without skipping a beat. "It is natural that so much flying activity would cause suspicion. PFIB would always visit the house we own 25 miles or so from here because someone reported us at one point. I don't know how they knew it was us, but since the only address we are tied to is an old house, they came to that. Ever since, we have just been on their radar."

"So, this house is illegal?" Ember asked cracking a smile.

"Oh yes, very much so," laughed Drake. "We don't have to pay taxes, so yes."

He put the breakfast on the table and everyone gathered around to eat.

"However, the events that took place last night put me and Jane on their target list. We are no longer safe," Drake sighed.

"You can come with us," Ember said. "I am sure that Cadell and Dalka won't mind. It is the least we can do for you."

Jane cast a glance over at her husband and looked at Ember. "You really think so?"

"I am almost certain!" Ember said.

"I know I don't mind," Jack added raising his fork as he spoke. "Ember and I will talk to the dragons when they return from their hunt. I am sure it will not be a problem."

When the group was done eating, Ember decided that she was ready to turn on her phone. While she was in town, Jane was kind enough to buy her a charger. Ember had put it in her pocket seeing it was easier than carrying it in a bag. She turned on her phone, swiping past the hundreds of missed calls and text from her mother and friends. There was one text however that caught her eye. It was one from her father and it simply read: *I am sorry. Please come home.*

She shook her head and deleted the text, overcome with a wave of emotions. She decided to return to the barn to wait for her friends in order to clear her mind. But when she got there, she found them already back.

"Well that was quick," she said when she walked in. She noticed the uneasy look on the dragons' faces as soon as she walked in."

"We didn't go," Cadell stated simply.

"What? Why? Aren't you hungry?" Ember asked confused.

"Of course, we are hungry! Don't you think that we would go and eat if we could?" Cadell snapped.

"Cadell!" Dalka snarled angrily. "Enough!"

Ember watched as Cadell bent his head as he tried to deal with his emotions. She then looked up at Dalka, hoping that she would give her a calmer answer.

"The plague has infected the deer here," Dalka almost whispered. "It's here too."

"How do you know?" Ember asked.

"You can smell it Ember, you can smell it," Dalka said. Ember could see that the dragon was growing distraught. "It is a smell I will never forget and I swear it will haunt me for the rest of my life. The island reeks of it."

"Ok, we need to remain calm." Ember tried her best to soothe her friend.

"Calm? Calm? Oh, that is just so easy," Cadell snarled sarcastically.

"Guys!" Ember said, taking on a stern, authoritative voice. She allowed her body language to show that she was no longer taking no for an answer. "Get outside!"

Both dragons looked at Ember slightly confused but walked out.

"Now take a breath and chill out!" Ember said

exasperated. She began to walk into the woods and the dragons followed suit. She found a small clearing where they could all rest comfortably.

"Just take a minute and think. We will figure this out. Just breathe."

Both dragons did as they were told and remained quiet for a moment.

"Yeah Ember, that helped a lot. Maybe breathing will cure the disease right out of the deer too," Cadell joked angrily.

Before Ember could even realize what was happening, Dalka lunged at Cadell, gripping his shoulder with her strong jaws and slamming him to the ground. She grabbed his neck and stood growling over top of him. Ember began to feel her energy draining as Cadell began to take energy. She tried to block him out but he was too strong for her. The shield that she had tried to put up was torn down like paper. His markings glowed dangerously bright, bathing everything in an eerie blood red light.

He pushed off the turquoise dragon, throwing her into a tree as he rose to his feet. A bone rattling growl erupted from his throat as he stalked over to Dalka, still dazed as she tried to get to her feet. The way he stalked over to Dalka, Ember knew Cadell was about to kill her.

"Cadell!" Ember cried out. "Stop! You're hurting me!"

Cadell immediately stopped and looked around him. All his markings immediately ceased glowing when he heard Ember's strained voice. Ember was on the ground, too weak to stand and when he laid eyes on her, the realization hit the dragon and Ember saw it. Dalka was still trying to get to her feet by the base of the tree. She had a deep cut on her face.

Blood fell from Cadell's wounds as he backed away in shock. She knew that both dragons did wrong, but she was not going to place blame yet.

"Are you both okay?" Ember called, her voice raspy as she tried to stand.

"I...I..." Cadell bent his head and closed his eyes, muscles flexing and retracting in confusion.

Shaking his large head, he roared and jumped in the sky and took off, sending dust blowing around. Ember coughed and saw Dalka limping over to her.

"Are you alright, little one?" she said gently bending her head.

"What did you do?" Ember asked angrily. She was now going to place blame.

Dalka bent her head, ashamed. Emerald eyes glowing in sadness.

"Why did you attack him?"

"I'm sorry, Ember."

Ember managed to stand and continued to yell at the dragon. She let all the anger and fear she had kept bottled up pour out.

"You are both so petty! Asking a teenager for help because of a prophecy! I mean, my life at home wasn't so great, but I mean, at least I am not playing babysitter for 8-ton idiots! Now he is gone, Dalka. My partner is gone because you can't control your anger!"

"Control my anger?" Dalka said dangerously calm. "The times that I wanted to kill your race and never did, because I thought of how it would scar you. I controlled my anger for far too long. Your race killed my child. Took the one thing that I loved the most in my life. And you want to talk to me about controlling anger?" Dalka's voice was filled with harsh venom, but it never lifted into a yell.

Ember didn't say anything, but instead turned and left, leaving the conversation to hang precariously in the air.

16

Ember really didn't know where she was going. She just needed to clear her head and the only thing she could think of was walking through the woods. She followed a trail, thinking and fuming. The occasional bird would fly from a bush and startle her, making her even more angry because she wasn't prepared. She found a creek that ran through the woods and bent down. She watched the fish swim and it calmed her nerves slightly.

She wasn't sure what pushed her to do it, but without thinking she slipped her hands into the cool stream. The water slipped over her fingers, it was ice cold, but it began to grow warm. The water around her fingers turned blue and the fish scattered. Suddenly an image appeared. A woman, alongside a young dragon hatchling. It was red with scattered white spots, as if he was splattered with white paint.

Suddenly, Ember remembered who the dragon was.

Zimmeran, Dalka's son.

She could only guess that the woman who was next to the dragon was Martha. She didn't know why she was seeing them, but she didn't dare withdraw her hand from the water.

She watched the scene unfold on the image in the water. There were no sounds or words, but they were not needed.

The hatchling was jumping and playing in the woods while Martha watched. He chased a butterfly, curiosity getting the better of him. He jumped up and caught the butterfly between his talons. Ember flinched. She knew the butterfly wouldn't have survived it.

When the dragon opened his talons, he expected the butterfly to be alive and fluttering about, but he saw a crushed, twitching and broken one instead. Its wings were torn and legs bent in angles. Zimmeran's face fell and Ember could see the smoke that escaped his nostrils.

Martha came over with a grim look on her face and smiled sadly at the dragon. In size, Martha just reached Zimmeran's shoulder. She took the butterfly and Zimmeran ran off into the woods. Martha gently scooped up a loose patch of soil and placed the crippled butterfly into the newly created hole. Zimmeran returned moments later carrying a small stone, he seemed proud of his discovery.

Walking over to the small pile of dirt, he placed the rock gently on top of it and backed away from it. The scene then panned to show the rest of the clearing. Within it, Ember saw hundreds of small mounds with rocks on top of them.

The scene blurred, and then Zimmeran and Martha were by the barn back at Jack's house. Martha had a toy butterfly in her hand and was tossing it in the air. She would catch it gently. She tossed it to the awaiting dragon who caught it, when he opened his talons, the toy was shredded. Martha sadly smiled and took the shredded toy away.

The scene blurred once more, this time Martha and Zimmeran were back in the clearing. Another butterfly was fluttering around the clearing. Unlike the first time Ember saw him try and catch the butterfly, his approach was slower and full of caution. He gently swiped up the butterfly, the motion seeming practiced. When he opens his talons, he saw that the butterfly was sitting alive and well in the center. He looked up at Martha with a happy expression. She came over and clapped happily, embracing Zimmeran. The butterfly fluttered away unharmed and the scene faded from the water.

Ember sat on the bank of the creek, unsure how to comprehend what she just saw. She felt a mixture of sadness, awe, and confusion. Why had it showed her that? What did it mean? Shaking her head, she got to her feet and walked back to Drake and Jane's home.

The trek back was longer than Ember had expected. She had to admit she was grateful. She didn't really want to face Dalka or Cadell after everything that had happened. She wondered if they would be mad at her, or if they would still be mad at each other. But none of that would even matter if the dragons weren't there.

Ember couldn't help but worry slightly. What if the dragons never came back? What if Cadell flew away and never returned? What if they never wanted to see her again? Her mind was flooded with anxieties and unanswered fears, but her mind could not provide any answers that would soothe them.

On her way, she heard the faint *thump, thump, thump,* of an approaching chopper. Her heart sank and her mind whirled into panic. Her slow pace turned into a full-blown run. Her legs pumped and her lungs burned. Sometimes her torso would overrun her legs and she would trip and fall.

Dusting herself off, she ignored the stinging in her legs and continued.

She heard yelling when she reached the house and immediately stopped near the edge of the woods. She peered through and her mouth went dry. About a dozen armored vehicles surrounded the house and barn, and a chopper hovered above, sending ripples of wind across the freshly mowed lawn.

"Let go of me!" Jane's voice screamed from the house.

"I swear if you do anything to my wife, I will personally see that your ass is dead!" Drake said angrily from the same direction.

She felt something grab her arm and she almost screamed before a hand covered her mouth, muffling it. She struggled until she heard a voice by her ear.

"Shh! Ember, stop! It's me!" she heard Jack say.

He let her go and Ember turned to face him.

"What are you doing here?" she whispered.

"I came to find you and the dragons," he replied. "But we need to go and find them now! Drake and Jane need help!"

She knew what was happening and listened to Jack. Ember ran on still burning legs with Jack on her heels to the clearing of the woods where she had last seen Cadell and Dalka. She jumped over fallen logs and ducked under low-lying branches before skidding to a halt in the middle of the clearing where she found nothing. Jack came up a few moments behind her, hindered by his age.

The clearing was completely empty.

She couldn't yell for them, as it would give away her cover. What hope she had had to save her friends completely melted as hysteria blossomed from the pits within. Tears sprung from her eyes, her breaths began to be stolen from her, the world seemed to spin.

"Where are they?" Jack asked, clearly as stressed as the girl was.

"I don't know!" she cried, panicked.

She ran blindly back to the house tripping over everything in her path, the tears coming down so fast she couldn't wipe them away to see the trail ahead of her. Her hands burned from the impact of the ground as she tried to break her falls, and her clothes were ripped from the branches that tried to stop her way like needy hands.

She and Jack managed to reach the house again, and saw that the house and barn had been completely destroyed. Out in the yard lay two bodies. Nothing moved. Everything was silent except for the pounding of Ember's heart.

She walked into the yard. There were dozens of tire tracks from where the vehicles had been and she could see ruts where they had gotten stuck in the moist ground. She approached the bodies and saw the blond hair of Jane covered in scarlet red that was seeping from a small hole in her head. She was face down, dress drenched in mud and torn. Drake, who was next to his wife was also face down. He too had the similar bullet hole to that of his wife. Ember clenched her fist and squeezed her eyes shut as sobs racked her body.

"Oh, my God," Jack whispered. "Ember, we have to get out of here. We cannot stay here."

"You're damn right you can't," said a voice from the trees behind them.

Ember turned to see that it was the agent that had tried

to kill her back in Jack's barn. He had a gun pointed directly at Ember. She felt Jack jump in front of her just as the agent pulled the trigger. She felt no pain and was confused at first.

And then she saw Jack fall.

Jack!

The man she had known slightly less than the dragons, yet felt like she had known him her whole life. He was like the father she once had, taking her under his wing, loving her, caring for her, forgiving her. Ember sobbed as she dropped down by the old man's head.

"What did you do?" Ember screamed, her voice reaching to the point of hysteria. It echoed through the woods around her and clawed her throat. "What the hell did you DO!"

Ember screamed, allowing the demon to come unleashed from her soul, crying into the air for the things it had lost.

"You know, I wanted to get you. Now that I think about it though, you may be useful. Guess it's lucky that fossil of a human got in the way, huh, at least it wasn't a loss," Penser said, clearly not caring about the teen who sat screaming in anguish in front of him.

"Ember," the old man rasped.

"You're alive! Let me see if I can heal you!" Ember sputtered out, ignoring Penser who had the gun now aimed at her.

"Move over from the man!" The PFIB agent screamed. "I thought you were dead! I need to make sure you stay dead!"

She didn't oblige him and was confused why he didn't shoot her. She placed her hand on Jack's stomach and pulled forth the energy as if she was trying to heal one of the dragons, but she found that it wasn't working. When she pulled back her hand, she found that it was covered in warm, sticky blood. It oozed from her fingers, dropping back on Jack's torso, reeking of metal.

"Jack! Jack!" Ember said pushing her hair back, getting the blood within it.

"Run," Jack choked.

"I am not leaving you," Ember whimpered out.

"I said move!" Penser yelled shooting the gun.

Ember saw the gun had been moved into the air. She realized it was a warning shot, the man did not want to kill her. He must have thought that she had some value.

Jack looked up at Ember, not needing to hold her hand because he already held her heart. "I love you, my dear. You were the child I never had. If Martha could have seen you…" His voice gave out as blood poured from his mouth and onto the grass. His eyes glazed over and his breathing once shallow, became nonexistent.

She hugged Jack's neck, hardly able to breathe through the sobs that racked her body. She smelled the blood beneath her but ignored it. She couldn't leave him. Her mind was unable to comprehend what was happening.

Ember heard the thumping of wings and turned to see Dalka in the clearing. She saw the look on her face turn from shock into sheer rage. Dalka saw Penser and charged the man.

"*I WILL KILL THEM ALL!*" she roared, fire erupting from her mouth and into the air above.

Suddenly gunfire erupted from the trees and men came pouring out. Grenades were thrown at the dragon and smoke filled the clearing. She saw the dragon roar out in pain and fall.

"Dalka!" she cried out to her friend.

Ember coughed as the smoke entered her lungs and she was tackled to the earth. She felt hands roughly forcing her to the ground as sobs racked her body. Another roar sounded from above and fire came from the sky. She heard men screaming and felt them lifted off of her. She scrambled to her feet, still blinded by smoke.

She felt something pick her up from above and she began to struggle. She had to help Dalka.

"Stop struggling!" a familiar voice called from above.

Cadell, she realized. He came back.

She went limp and let the dragon fly her to wherever he deemed fit. He landed roughly in the middle of the woods and she tumbled out of his talons. He turned to take off again before Ember stood up and shouted after him.

"Wait! Don't just leave me here!" she sobbed.

"I am not! Just stay here and hide, I will be back!"

Before Ember could argue, Cadell took off into the sky, leaving Ember alone in the clearing still covered in the blood of her dead friend.

CHAPTER
17

All Ember could do was sit against a tree and think. Her mind lost into itself as the sun faded behind the clouds, plunging the world into a familiar, welcome darkness. Bugs crawled up and down Ember's arms, but she never bothered to brush them off.

It was a trap. She realized. *They killed Jane and Drake, both innocent people. They killed Jack while trying to kill me. I should have known that they wouldn't have just left them there. It would have been too easy to trace. Jack was not kidding when he said that they could get away with murder if they really wanted to.*

But there is still one question that I don't understand.

How did they find us?

Ember breathed heavily as she reached in her pocket for her phone to check the time. When she pulled it out, a realization hit her.

The phone! The phone led them. As soon as I turned it on at Jack's house they came, the day after I turned it on at Drake and Jane's, they came. I am the reason they are all dead. This is all my fault.

Ember realized that the odd men in the store back when she was at Jack's made sense.

They followed us back from my house, I don't know how but they did. They found us, planted something in the charger in my phone. It all makes sense!

Ember angrily grabbed her phone, taking her dirt-ridden nails and digging them into the metal.

"You damn thing!" she said as the tears stained her face. She threw it onto the ground and crushed it with her foot. The anger and sadness she felt was taken out on the device. She picked up the shattered phone and chucked it against a tree, screaming as the guilt gripped her.

Ember brought her knees to her chest and allowed herself to cry.

All my fault.

The sound of wings beating brought her back to reality as Cadell landed in the clearing. She looked up at him, feeling the hair stick to her hot face. His face was grim and somber, but it was hard to tell much else in the dim moonlight.

"Are you hurt?" her partner asked her.

"Not physically. What about Dalka? Jack?" Ember questioned, her voice raw and scratchy from smoke and hoarse from crying.

The dragon dipped his head and his blue eyes closed.

"All bodies were gone, Dalka is gone. I cannot be sure if she is dead."

"Are you sure she is gone?" Ember pleaded, she was hoping, trying, holding on to anything.

"She wasn't there. I looked everywhere. I saw the tracks where she got up and left. She escaped, but she was bleeding profusely. With the amount of blood I saw, I do not know if she was able to find a safe place to rest. We cannot go after her now, it is too dangerous. We can see if we can track her down when morning comes."

"This is all my fault," Ember cried out.

The girl began pacing as she tried to convince herself that everything that happened wasn't true.

"Ember, stop. You need to pull yourself together! I can't do this without you, we need to work together and get through this!" Cadell begged.

Ember did not hear him and continued to pace.

Growing impatient, Cadell roughly grabbed the girl and pressed her against a tree.

"Get a grip!" he yelled at her. "We *will* get through this, okay?"

He dropped the shocked girl back on the ground where she sunk against the tree with her head in her hands. The dragon sighed and his markings began to glow. She felt energy being poured into her and she knew that it was Cadell's way of trying to comfort her. He settled down on the ground and Ember walked over to him, leaning against his shoulders.

"Get some rest," he sighed, smoke visibly puffing from his nostrils in the moonlight that was filtered from the trees. "I will keep watch."

"I can't sleep," Ember whimpered. "I can't get them out of my head. You were right, I wasn't ready."

She felt Cadell sigh again. He turned his large head to look at the girl.

"When the plague started, I couldn't either. There were thousands of dead bodies everywhere. You couldn't fly without seeing at least one on a good day. There were nights I and the group of dragons I lived with would stay awake for days, unable to sleep. Haunted by the images of once alive and healthy dragons, living life and having a family of their own, now suddenly dead. Every ounce of life gone. What once was a being, with a personality, story, a life of its own was now only food for maggots. There would be someone who remembered them, but they too would die, and the memories would die with them.

"Even though we claimed to be tough dragons, the thoughts haunted us. I don't think it was the unholy sight as much as it was the fear of death, fearing that we too would end up like that. We finally figured out a solution. We would take turns telling each other stories. When the idea was first introduced, it was brushed aside by the majority, but when most of us became sleep deprived, it was tried out of desperation.

"Surprisingly, it worked quite well. I, however, became the favorite for telling the stories," the dragon mused. "I know that it is bound to work the same for humans too. We aren't so different, are we?"

Ember yawned and shook her head as thunder rumbled in the distance.

Cadell sighed and shifted himself to a more comfortable position.

"Many years ago, long before you or anyone you know today was ever born, dragons and humans worked together. Side by side, the two races succeeded together, learning and thriving alongside each other. This was back before your kind had any means of photography or good documentation. That is why you believed we were just lore.

"Our king and queen before Amrendra loved humans, they cherished our relationship with them. However, there was one group of dragons on the island who didn't like the humans."

Cadell stopped and hung his head low, eyes glazed over, shameful.

"That was my friends and I. We didn't like them. We felt as if we should rule the world, and that the humans shouldn't be on this planet. We created the mean face of dragons that is in your books. We were the group of dragons that set cities on fire, killed innocent people."

"Why?" Ember asked shocked. "Why would you do that?"

"I was angry," Cadell stated simply. "And it was something that I could control. I was angry because I wasn't going to be leader, I was angry about everything."

Cadell shook his large head and looked out onto the horizon, watching the distant lightning play in the sky.

"I regret it now. I didn't regret it then, but I do now. I killed the very thing that is going to save my race from extinction. It's funny how the tables have turned. I feel guilty, but I know that I can't go back and change what I did, nor will I ever be able to. I can't seem to forgive myself, and I don't think I ever will."

Cadell tilted his head to Ember.

"If anyone would have told me that I would be risking my life for a human girl, I would have never believed them. I still hate humans to be honest, but I like you and I liked Jack." Cadell's eyes closed gently. "It is funny how such a small creature can be capable of so much change."

Ember leaned against the dragon and realized that her

partner was a killer. Yet, she could not bring herself to hate him or be angry with him.

At this point in her life, nothing seemed to faze or surprise her anymore. What really mattered to her was that he learned, and he was growing. He was becoming a better dragon because of his mistakes, and he was paying the price for his actions. She patted her friend's shoulder, resting her head on his muscular outstretched leg.

"It is what it is," Ember said tiredly. "You live, you learn, you move on."

"Yes," Cadell said. "Sadly, I still need to learn how to do that."

A sudden rumble of thunder abruptly interrupted Cadell and he glanced down at the girl who was slowly drifting off to sleep next to him. He angled his wing so the rain would not get her wet. The rain gently pattering against Cadell's wings lulled Ember into sleep.

· · · · · ·

Ember awoke next to Cadell, the sun was shining around them, reflecting the thousands of water droplets that lay dormant on the grass and leaves. The patch of ground below where Ember laid was dry, she had to guess that Cadell had kept her dry through most of the storm.

Cadell was awake when she began to stir and tipped his head to her.

"Morning, kid," he greeted. "How are you feeling?"

"I don't know," Ember sighed, rubbing her eyes as the events from the day prior flooded back to her.

Cadell stood, shaking off the water that was still on his scales. "Come, we have a long flight ahead of us."

"No, you don't," said a voice from the bushes. Penser

and dozens of men stepped from the clearing, aiming guns at the pair. "Give it up, dragon, one word against us and I can shoot the girl faster than you can reach her."

Cadell's eyes grew tense, but he knew he was outmatched.

"You screwed up, dragon. You let your guard down," Penser drawled. "Come with me without a struggle and I will let you both live."

"I will never go with you!" Ember hollered.

"Enough. You will go with them," Cadell rumbled from above her.

"What?" Ember asked shocked, looking up at her friend.

Cadell didn't meet the girls gaze. "Obey me."

Ember did. The tone of his voice told her that he knew what was going to be best for them. She raised her hands in surrender and the soldiers lowered their weapons.

"Aren't we going to have fun?" Penser said as he raised a small handheld radio. "Come on in boys, we got 'em right where we want them."

18

Ember didn't remember what had happened in the clearing, only that she and Cadell had guns raised at them and they looked different from normal. When they went off, everything went black. When Ember awoke, she rubbed her eyes still foggy with sleep and looked around the room she was in. It looked like a high-end prison.

She was in a beige room, but she saw that the paint was painted on lightly, as specks of darker brown showed beneath. There was one barred window and a white bolted door. A toilet and a sink sat in the corner, and across from that next to her bed sat a small oak drawer. She sat on top of a bed that was made with white sheets and white pillows. Everything in the room was dull.

Heaving herself up on aching arms, she walked to the window and looked down. She saw snow falling on the pavement many stories below. A city rose faintly behind a horizon of trees, but that provided no clues for Ember to help figure out where she was.

She heard the bolts on the door move and she watched as an older soldier brought in a lunch dish. She knew by the look on his face that he was not friendly, nor did he like her.

"I want this eaten and gone in 45 minutes. We will be coming here to take you out for questioning. I don't care if you are ready or not."

With that, he briskly walked out of the room and slammed the door, leaving Ember with a steaming tray of what she had first thought was breakfast. When she peered closer, she saw that it consisted of potatoes, carrots, and soup, clearly lunch.

How long have I been asleep? Ember thought as she played with the spoon on the tray.

With no appetite, Ember left the food untouched. She decided to toss the food in the toilet seeing there were no cameras in the room. She found that very odd, but she let it go.

She laid on the bed, closing her eyes in hope she would fall back asleep and escape the fear she felt inside. She was too tired to cry, so she chose instead to feel all the emotions inside her. The door's bolts moved again and Ember looked up to see Penser alongside the older soldier who had given her lunch and a few older men with guns slung across their chest. She also spotted a young soldier who stood hesitantly behind the rest. The look he gave her wasn't mean, Ember's guess was maybe sympathy, but she did not know for sure.

"Ah! Look, Sleeping Beauty has awakened!" said Penser in a sickeningly sweet voice. "Come now, there are things that I want to know."

Ember fought back the bile that rose in her throat. She hated him. She did not argue and followed behind him. She was trailed by the guards and a younger man. She was led down a hallway where she began to hear faint noises coming from below. It was a deep baritone and she knew it was Cadell's.

"*LET ME GO!*" she heard the dragon shout angrily.

The venom in his voice sent chills down her spine. The times that she had thought Cadell was angry, he was merely agitated. Ember heard him curse everything in every cuss word she had ever heard and then some. Her heart longed to go and see Cadell, to help him and to calm him down.

"Your dragon friend has been quite the handful," Penser said, his voice strained. "He has refused everything until we let him see you. I figured we could do the questioning with you two together, should be interesting to see what happens when I play my cards."

Ember fought back the urge to curl up her fist and sock the man in the head. She knew if she tried to do anything, the guards behind her would put a bullet through her head. She decided that painting a mental image of Cadell tearing apart the man would have to do for the current situation.

They approached a stairwell and Ember hesitated, not wanting to go any further. She was shoved harshly down the stairs where she fell face first. Her arms were not able to block her fall fast enough and she hit her nose harshly on the hard stairs. She scrambled to her feet as her eyes watered in pain. She grabbed her nose as blood gushed from it. Blood dripped on the floor and Penser looked back disgustedly at the girl. He shook his head and they continued to walk down the stairs as Ember clutched her bleeding nose.

They entered a large room that was sectioned off down the middle with metal bars like a jail cell. On the other side of the bars, Cadell paced with his neck snaking and his tail flicking. When he saw Ember come down the steps holding her nose, he ran as near as he could get to her, snout sticking out of the bars in her direction.

"Ember!" he cried out. "What happened? What did he do to you?"

"Don't answer him," Penser snapped at Ember. He roughly grabbed her hand and dragged her to a chair. It didn't look like a normal chair. It was unfamiliar to her and she leaned away from it. Suddenly two of the guards came up behind her and pushed her into the chair, putting her arms and legs into straps as she struggled to get away.

Something was put to her head and it shocked her. Ember yelled out in pain, the scream cutting her throat like glass. Cadell roared from the other side of the bars, markings glowing. The shock coursed through her body, and every ounce of her being. She could feel nothing but the pain the chair gave her.

"Stop!" Ember pleaded. "Please stop!"

She didn't care what she had to do, but the pain became so tremendous she could no longer bear it. The shock died down and Ember sat in the chair slumped over, recovering. She panted trying to catch her breath and all her muscles spasmed from the electric shock. Cadell's deep growls could be heard reverberating around the room. She could feel him pushing energy into her and she did not try and stop him. She felt almost fully recovered after a few seconds.

"Now that you have a taste of what this can do, it would be best if you told us everything that has happened over the past few weeks."

Ember's face turned into a rough scowl and Cadell's already deep growl deepened. She knew that if Cadell continued to give her energy, she would be able to withstand a lot more than the average human.

"If you think that I am going to tell you anything, you are sadly mistaken," Ember snapped.

Penser grinned dangerously and Ember knew that he would be more than willing to kill her if it came down to it.

"Have it your way then." Penser said holding a remote.

He pressed a button on it and the shock started back up again, starting dull and then coming full force. She felt like it was tearing her apart and she screamed as the pain went through her. It died down again and she sat breathing. Her nose was still bleeding, running down her face and onto the front of her clothes, staining them scarlet. She felt Cadell push more energy to her, helping her to regain her strength. Ember guessed that while she was in pain, she must have set up a mental block because Cadell ceased giving energy to her when the shock started. She suspected that it was also affected by distance. She had to see Cadell in order to give and take energy and touch him in order to heal him.

"Do you want to tell me now?" Penser asked, tone uncaring as he nonchalantly tossed the remote from hand to hand.

Ember coughed and shook her head. She didn't want to die, but she also couldn't reveal the dragons' secret. Before Penser could push the button again, a hot gust of air and flame rushed past Ember and burned Penser and the remote. She heard Penser shout and jump back, dropping the burning remote and moving away from the dragon.

Cadell stood rumbling as he finished his large blast of flame. His neck was curved and chest was puffed out. He met Ember's eyes and he nodded abruptly with a snort.

The guards shot darts at the dragon and he fell to the ground with a loud *thump!*

Ember was also shot with darts and became too weak to comprehend what was happening. She began to fade in and out of consciousness until she was ripped from the chair and shoved to stand. A guard grabbed her roughly by the arm and led her up the stairs. She was dazed; everything felt like a dream to her. Sounds were distorted and her vision blurry. The girl wanted to collapse and she didn't know how much longer that her muscles could keep her on her feet.

When she was shoved into her room, she stumbled over to her bed where she managed to hit the mattress before succumbing to sleep.

· · · · ·

Ember awoke to her sheets covered in blood. She was confused and pulled back away in shock from all the red. It was everywhere, on the pillows, comforter and sheets. It was all over her shirt and when she looked in the mirror, she saw her face covered in the sticky red substance.

She walked over to the sink and washed the dried blood from her face. She was relieved to see that her nose had stopped bleeding. She did the best she could with the soap provided to her to wash her shirt, but she didn't want to risk getting it too wet. Ember didn't know how the people of PFIB would react to having the sheet ruined, but she could only hope for a cruel batch of people they were somewhat understanding of her situation.

Drying everything off the best she could, Ember saw that it was dark outside and returned to her bed where she sat on the side not ruined. She felt lucky that she had been asleep most of the time. While asleep, her mind wouldn't think and it wouldn't haunt her. Now not tired and having nothing to occupy her mind, she had nothing left to do except sit and think.

Her mind began to trod into the depths of everything that had happened. The image of Jack laying helpless in the clearing always came back to her mind in vivid detail and she closed her eyes trying to stop the tears from escaping. She tried to calm herself by thinking that wherever Jack's soul went to, he was happy. He must be with his wife and their adopted dragon son, and it made Ember smile slightly thinking about them all together again. She thought about Dalka, and realized that she may still be alive and it gave her hope.

Her mind then wondered to the vision and then to the island of dragons that Ember still had to save. She was lost, confused, scared, and hurt. She didn't know how she was going to complete the prophecy. The door opened, jarring her from her thoughts and the young soldier entered again with clothes and bed sheets. He was the young man who followed behind them earlier. He seemed only a little older than Ember, and he seemed kind. Ember decided to take a shot in the dark.

"Can you...can you help me?" Ember asked.

"I don't know, I am sorry," the man said as his eyes flickered with hesitation.

Ember found herself suddenly hoping. He seemed to not want what was happening. Maybe with enough convincing, she could get him sided with her. She thanked God for the stroke of luck that made her ask the soldier to help her.

"I do not agree with what they are doing. All I can tell you is that your dragon friend is fine," he said. Ember guessed it was the look on her face that got him to continue talking.

Not satisfied with his answer and wanting to pull him more, she moved over to the other side of the room where she eyed him warily.

"I won't hurt you," the soldier said as he set the clothes on top of the wooden dresser. "I am not like the rest of them," he admitted, scratching the back of his head.

He stripped the sheets off the bed and threw the old ones by the door alongside the old pillowcases. Ember stayed silent and watched him intently. When he finished changing the bed, he outstretched his hand to her.

"I am Chase," he said as Ember cautiously slipped her small hand into his muscular one. She knew playing the hard-to-get card would work.

"Ember," she said withdrawing her hand and letting it fall back to her side.

"Well it is nice to know your name," he said flashing her a smile. "They always referred to you as 'the girl' so I never heard your name."

Ember just stayed quiet. *Come on, dude.* She thought. She knew if she stayed distant enough and looked sad enough, she would be able to get this guy to help her. Even having him in the room with her for a couple of minutes, she already knew how she needed to play the game.

Chase's smile faded seeing her sad face and he looked at her dead in the eyes.

"Did you kill people in cold blood?" he asked.

"No!" Ember said shocked. "Well, I haven't. My friend did in the past, but he learned. And recently he did it to protect me."

"Did you kill Santa?" Chase questioned.

Ember was at a loss for words but she shook her head and held the bridge of her nose. "What is your point?"

"I don't see a reason for you and the dragon to be locked up here, so I am going to help you escape."

Gotcha!

CHAPTER
19

Chase was good, really good. He knew how to sneak her extra food, clothes, anything she really needed. He was also excellent at acting, pretending to hate her and intimidate her around the other officers. She found that he was in training, and that was why he followed her everywhere and got the lousy job of caring for her. The only thing that he asked in return was that she did not let anyone in the facility know that he was helping her. It could get Chase and her killed if anyone found out about the forbidden alliance.

When he would come to give her food or clothes, they would talk. There was no camera in the room so they could talk about their plan without fear of being found.

"Why are you helping me?" she asked him a week after her arrival at the building.

He smiled sadly. "This isn't what I wanted to do with my life. This was what my father wanted. He always went on about this story how some great, great, great, grandfather's family was all killed in a fire started by a dragon. Ever since, every man that was born in my family joined this group. I, however, really don't want to kill the dragons. I see them as beautiful creatures. I read a book about them once in a library, and ever since then, I kind of just became fascinated by them. I knew they were real because of my father, but I had a hard time believing they were evil."

Ember nodded, she understood how he viewed them.

"I remember the first time I saw a dragon. The agency had caught it. It was my first day and I had walked in unnoticed when no one was in the room. I talked to this dragon and it told me about this prophecy and how it was trying to find this girl. I felt so bad for it. All I wanted to do was set it free and help it. So, whenever I could, I would sneak it food. I tried so hard to come up with some escape plan, but they killed it before I could." Chase seemed incredibly sad, as if the event affected him more than he let on.

"How long were you friends with the dragon?" Ember asked.

"About a year," Chase admitted.

"There was a lot more that happened, wasn't there?" Ember asked quietly.

"Yes. I don't want to talk about this right now. But I am doing this for her."

Ember looked at Chase. She had only known Cadell and Dalka for not even half as long and the pain of possibly losing Dalka still was like a crushing weight.

"I am part of that prophecy, as crazy as it sounds. I have to help them. I have come so far, and lost two of my best friends along the way," Ember said. Her voice grew thick with emotion as she thought about Dalka and Jack.

"I am sorry for your loss," said Chase as he stood up.

"I am sorry for your loss too," said Ember.

Chase sighed. "I guess I am doing this to give myself a peace of mind. I'm doing this for Atlas."

"Was that the dragon's name?" Ember asked.

Chase smiled sadly as he got up and opened the door. "Yes."

Chase took one look back at Ember and then looked down the hallway. His face scrunched up in fake anger after giving her a wink.

"Stupid girl!" Chase shouted as two guards entered the room.

"What did she do?" one of the men asked, peering over at Chase curiously.

"I can't even," Chase spat. "What are you here for?"

"We fixed the remote that the damn dragon burned," said the other guard. "We are taking her back down to be questioned more."

Chase's face noticeably paled before he pulled himself together. He seemed to forget the chair, but Ember had not. Ember wasn't moved from her room since Cadell had broken the remote and it made her anxious she was not able to see her friend. Even though Chase was able to tell her he was alright, it did not give her enough peace of mind to cease her worry. Apparently, they forgot that he breathed fire, which Ember did not know how that was possible to forget. Considering Cadell had killed at least 50 of their men with fire before their capture, Ember had to guess that it either was not brought to Penser's attention or the man was stupid.

Chase walked over and roughly grabbed Ember's arm and dragged her out of the door. She felt his head bend down by her ear when the guards were not looking.

"I will find a way to stop them from shocking you as much. I know it hurts," he murmured, hot breath against her ear. "Just hold on."

She nodded silently and mentally noted to thank him for it later as he straightened himself back up and pushed her forward. She went down the stairs and Chase's grip tightened. He seemed to have remembered the fact she tripped down them the last time and almost broke her nose.

When she entered the room, she saw Cadell chained and mouth clamped shut by what seemed like a gigantic metal muzzle. He saw her and roused, trying to move over to her. The chains restricted his movement and groaned as he strained against them. She could see blood pooled all over the floor beneath him and she was hit with a sickening metallic smell the further she went in.

What did they do to him? Ember thought as her anger rose. *How dare they?*

Ember began to fight Chase's grip as she saw Penser in the corner of the room watching her with his arms crossed.

"What did you do to him!" Ember yelled at him angrily as Chase's grip became painfully tight around her arms.

"The question should be what did *you* do to him," Penser smiled darkly. "If you had not fought or screamed, we wouldn't be in this situation right now, and your dragon friend here wouldn't be wounded."

Ember's anger turned to rage. "How dare you blame this on me! You are in the wrong here! You murdered people and dragons and you have tortured both of us! This is all your fault!"

Penser just laughed and walked over to the girl, tipping her chin up with an index finger so she was forced to look at his grey eyes. "Girl, you gotta another thing coming if you think that's all we did."

The man dropped her chin and Ember couldn't control

her anger anymore. She spat in the man's face. His face twisted in anger as he wiped the saliva off.

Raising his hand, she felt Chase tense up behind her as Penser's hand collided with her cheek. The resounding slap echoed across the room crisply. She heard Cadell's muffled roars and the straining of the chains as he pulled against them. She felt Cadell put energy into her and she put up a wall to block him. She knew he needed to keep his energy. She could feel him trying to push past her barrier, but she held strong.

"Put her in the chair," Penser snarled dangerously at Chase before walking over to retrieve the remote from a small place on the wall.

Chase put Ember in the chair and she struggled to get away. The two guards who had entered her room came over to help Chase as he tried to stop the struggling girl. When they managed to get her in the chair, she felt the familiar shock and screamed out as it intensified. She didn't remember how long it went on as she begged them to stop, but no matter how much she pleaded, they wouldn't.

When it finally died down, Ember was sobbing heavily, the tears clouding her vision and her breathing not able to take in enough air to support her. She felt Cadell give her energy and she allowed it, begging for anything to help soothe the pain. She could briefly see that Chase was no longer in the small group of soldiers anymore before more tears blocked her vision again.

"Tell me about the dragons!" she heard Penser from beside her.

Unable to muster up any voice, Ember just shook her head. She felt the shock once more and braced for it to become unbearable. But before it could begin intensifying, it suddenly stopped and she heard the sounds of electrical equipment dying all around her. Everything was plunged into darkness. Some emergency lights kicked on, bathing all the room's occupants in a dull, pale light.

"What the...?" Penser said, confused.

Ember let out a sigh of relief. Whatever Chase did, it worked. She heard footsteps coming down the stairs.

"What happened?" Chase's voice echoed from the stairwell. "Did you short out the power again, boss?"

"No!" Penser. "Come downstairs and stay with the girl while we go try and fix it."

Ember saw Chase approach as all the remaining soldiers left. She was still crying, but the tears were coming less often now.

"What did you do?" Ember hoarsely asked.

"I don't really know," said Chase chuckling a bit. "I went to the power room and cut a whole bunch of wires. I almost got electrocuted in the process, but I did it!"

Ember managed to let out a weak laugh and the two settled into a silence. Ember was slumped over, breathing hard, her body in pain and her chest heavy. Ember cracked an eye at Chase who was watching Cadell while the dragon watched Chase back.

"I don't think he likes me," Chase told the girl when he realized she was watching him.

"He just doesn't know that you are a friend," Ember said.

Cadell strained on the chains, his eyes full of pain as he tried to get closer to the girl.

"Cadell, stop!" Ember called. "You're hurting yourself. Save your strength!"

The dragon slowly stopped and gave Ember a sad look before settling down on the ground again.

"Have they fed him? Let him drink?" Ember asked concerned.

"No," said Chase sadly. "I can't help your friend. He is guarded at all times. I am sorry."

Ember looked over at the dragon who held her gaze with electric blue eyes. Chase helped her get out of the chair and led her to her room, being gentle with her since no other soldiers were around.

"I will tell Penser you were getting sick," said Chase as he softly closed the door behind them. "Although it's a good thing I have them occupied, not just to get you out of that chair, but also to talk to you. I have an idea to get you and your friend out of here," Chase said in a low voice.

"What would that be?" asked Ember, her hope rising.

"They need a guard for your friend during Christmas, so I will take that shift. There is barely anyone here during Christmas anyway, so I can unchain him and get you down to him. The room where he is being held has a large garage door; it was originally an old helicopter hangar, that's why it is so big and how we were able to fit him in," Chase explained. "I can open it and you two can fly away."

"When is Christmas?"

"Three days."

"But what about you?" asked Ember. "Do you want to come with us?"

Chase closed his eyes and shook his head. "I have a life here. I cannot leave."

Ember nodded her head and sat on the bed looking at him. She was going to miss him. He was the small ray of kindness and hope in the middle of hell.

"Will you be okay?" she asked after a moment of silence. "Will they know it was you?"

"Don't worry about that," Chase said with a tight smile. "Let me do this. Trust me. There are just some things you have to let go of so fate can take control."

They heard the voices of soldiers coming down the hallway before Chase flashed her a quick smile and slipped out of her room. When the door closed, she began to think about Christmas and what she was going to miss.

Christmas at her home, even when her father was drunk, wasn't bad. Since it was just her mother, father, and her, it was a small, but an emotionally-filling Christmas. Movies, twinkling lights, the gentle smell of peppermint laced with gingerbread, her home was *home* during Christmas. Her father seemed to cease drinking and was sober for a few days and her mom called off work. It was bliss to her.

The few weeks she had been with the dragons, trying to figure out what the prophecy really wanted from her flew past her fast. She thought back to her friends, their sacrifices, everything that they had done for her.

It was at that moment when she realized that one part of the prophecy had been fulfilled.

It wasn't me that needed to give up my life. I wasn't pure enough. But Jack was. He was not only that, but he gave up his life for me and the dragons. Jack was the person who remained pure, even after he lost his adopted son, even after he lost his wife, even after everything. And he never once suggested that he was the one. Ember's eyes closed in sorrow as she reflected. *Someone that was pure wouldn't have thought that they were so. Me thinking that I was the one to die made me not.*

Ember felt horrible. She felt selfish. She felt completely and utterly ashamed. She pulled herself up off the bed, emotions driving her to do something to keep her mind occupied. When her eyes rested on the sink, she got an idea.

She looked to see if it had something to stop the water from draining. When it didn't, she realized that she would have to improvise. She took toilet paper and wadded it up, stuffing it down the drain so that she would be able to hold water in the sink without it draining. She filled up the sink with water. When it reached the brim, she turned off the faucet. She hesitated before putting her hand in the water, listening to the leftover water drop in the sink from the faucet.

When she slipped her hands in the water, the tingling began and she looked to see what could be seen. When she saw Jack, she wanted to withdraw her hand, but she knew if she did it would go away. She saw him with Martha, and she saw Zimmeran. But the odd thing was that they were not at their home, or anywhere on earth.

She saw them playing in some sort of field. Hundreds of butterflies fluttering around them, landing on them as they laughed and played together. They are happy, Ember realized, and then something clicked.

This is what needed to happen, that is what she needed to see. She knew that the sacrifices that were made were required. Everything she was given in her life was because sacrifices were made. She knew the only way to save the dragons and restore peace was if people and dragons gave sacrifices. Although she didn't want that to happen, she knew it had to.

She saw Jack smiling, she saw Martha happy, and she

saw Zimmeran catching butterflies and letting them go. They were happy and they were safe, wherever they were. And for Ember, that was all she needed to know.

"I will save them. I swear it Jack, I will finish what you started. I will do it for you."

Two more days. Ember thought as she was led back down to the room with Cadell and the chair. *Two more days until we can put the plan into place and I can get out of here. The prophecy says that I will save them. I have to believe that I will.*

Instead of the chair that she was normally put into, a normal chair was there in the center of the room and she was pushed into it. She was facing Cadell's cage and she could see the dragon was in a lot of pain. *How long can they even go without food and water? Will he even be able to carry me come Christmas?*

She studied her friend as he strained against the chains trying to reach her. Breath heavy and labored, his markings glowed faintly as smoke poured from his nostrils. No matter how hard he tried, he could not make the chains budge.

"We have tried everything," Penser muttered. "We can't unmuzzle the dragon or he will burn us all alive, and I do not know how stupid people can be to not tell me that all of them breathe fire! So, we are going to try a new approach."

A handful of men entered Cadell's cage with prods, the ends crackled with electricity. She could not let Cadell get hurt.

"Do it to me! Please do it to me!" Ember cried out, but they would not listen.

They stabbed Cadell with the prods and the dragon jerked in pain, letting out a muffled roar. His eyes squeezed shut in pain and strained against the chains again. Ember tried her best to give him energy, but Cadell had built walls so strong Ember could not even dent them.

"What do you want? What do you want to know?" Ember cried out. "Just stop!"

Penser waved his hand and they stepped away from Cadell who stood breathing. The black dragon lifted his gaze and roared at Ember angrily. She understood that she wasn't to tell them anything.

"How do I get to their island?" Penser asked her.

She saw Cadell's eyes grow wide as he struggled against the chains.

DON'T TELL THEM. His eyes seemed to plead. *DON'T.*

"I don't know," Ember said playing the stupid approach.

"To hell you don't know!" spat Penser. "Shock him again."

"It isn't going to get you anywhere," Ember snarled. "Just give up."

"We never give up," Penser said shoving the chair she was in. "We are so close to getting all of those wretched creatures dead."

"What have they done to you?" Ember cried out.

"They killed my kid. That's what they did," Penser snarled out. "They shot down his helicopter. He was a Navy SEAL. I was his commander. Before he got shot down, he was on the radio with me. He told me that there were dragons, and everyone else that was with him confirmed it. I pinpointed his location before he went down. Do you know what it is like to hear your child dying? After that, I did research and figured out that almost every plane and chopper that went down, plus every ship that sank saw dragons.

"Now, I am going to make sure that no one loses their lives because of these wretched beasts," he spat angrily.

Ember watched the man as he struggled trying to control his emotions. She, however, felt no sympathy for him. "And you think that taking the lives of innocent human beings is going to help? Those creatures were only trying to protect themselves, and if you would take a step back, you would realize that what you're doing isn't solving anything."

Penser laughed. "I am doing the right thing. It is *you* that is doing wrong by helping them. They deserve to be dead. They deserve to die."

The men holding the prods pushed them into Cadell once more and the dragon tried his best to move away from the pain. The chains pushed into his scales causing more blood to pool around his feet and running down his body. Ember watched, begging them to stop, but they never ceased. When the dragon fell and stopped struggling Penser called the soldiers that were in the cage out with a wave of his hand and he left the room without a word.

Ember screamed at Cadell to get up, howling and crying until her throat was raw. The only soldier in the room with her was Chase. Ember gripped the bars with white knuckles as she cried. No matter how loud she screamed, her friend never moved and remained motionless as Chase dragged her away.

· · · · ·

Ember remained in her room for two days. She did not eat and only drank because the thirst became unbearable. She was left alone until Christmas Day came and Chase entered her room early in the evening with a bag. He smiled sadly at her. She could see he felt sorry for her and Ember knew she looked horrible.

"I will miss you," he told her as he handed her the bag. "You made my days here actually exciting."

"I will miss you too," she said as she took the bag. "You made hell somewhat livable."

He nodded and his face turned serious. "Alright, let's do this."

The duo turned and ran down the steps and Ember saw that Chase was right, there was really no one.

"Where does your family think you are?" Ember asked.

"I don't live with my family," said Chase. "Most soldiers take off because they are paid today, but some take jobs to keep busy."

Ember nodded and they entered the large room where Cadell stood in the chains. Ember had held her breath, expecting to see Cadell dead. When she saw the dragon up and moving, she ran to the bars in glee.

"Cadell!" Ember cried. She didn't hesitate now since no one was there to punish her.

He turned to her as Chase fumbled with the key to unlock one of the doors. She stepped inside with the bag on her back and began trying to undo the chains.

"Hold on, I have the key. Give me a second," Chase said as he jogged over to the dragon and the girl.

He stepped back when the dragon growled at him.

"It's okay, Cadell, he is going to help us escape," Ember

said patting her friend's shoulder gently.

Chase looked up at the dragon, and Ember could see he was still a bit nervous as he unlocked the chains. It was a lengthy process, then all that was left was the metal muzzle. Cadell lowered his head to Chase so he could unlock it and Cadell opened his mouth and roared, clearly happy to not be locked up.

"Shh!" Chase shushed him. "There are still people here!"

But his warning came too late. Alarms began to blare and Chase's face paled. He ran over and hit a button along the wall. The wall that was inside the cage began to open.

He was right. Ember thought. It was a door.

Cold air and snow filtered into the room causing her to shiver.

"Go!" yelled Chase.

Ember heard yelling and saw men filing down the steps, guns raised. They began to shoot and Cadell grabbed Ember in his talons and took off in the air. Ember turned and she saw Chase fall.

"Chase!" She shouted, but her voice was swept away from the wind.

"We are getting out of here, kid," Cadell called down. "I'll land when we are far enough away and let you get on my back before we make the long journey back to the island. I am spending no more time with your kind."

Ember saw vehicles chasing after them below, but with Cadell's speed, they were no match. The dragon flew faster and faster and they lost them in a matter of minutes. The wind flew by so quick that Ember found it hard to breathe. The cold air burned her skin; she only had a sweatshirt and jeans on. But she never complained.

Anything was better than being back there.

Cadell slowed down after what seemed to be hours, but could have only been a few minutes. He descended into a snow-covered forest and set the girl down. Ember turned and hugged Cadell, his blood getting all over her clothes, but she didn't care.

"I thought I lost you," she whimpered.

"I did too," he said as he wrapped his head gently around her.

The girl stepped back and looked over her friend.

"Are you okay? How badly are you injured?" Ember asked frantically, remembering the last time she saw him.

"I am fine," Cadell huffed. "Dragons are tougher than you think. But I am not worried about me. How are you? Did they harm you in anyway?"

"Only physically, what you saw in the chair," Ember replied.

"I am worried about your mental health, Ember," Cadell said. "I have been through a lot in my life, this is just another mountain. But you're just a hatchling, your mind has not seen as much as this."

"I am lucky to be alive," Ember said running her hands through her oily hair. She had not had a shower in a while, and was only able to wash herself with towels back in her room at the PFIB base. "But I am still worried about you. What about when they started shocking you? You fell!" Ember asked worried.

"I played dead," Cadell stated simply.

"I can't believe I didn't think about that," Ember said, kicking herself mentally. "I was so worried about you! Didn't you hear me screaming?"

"Yes, but I didn't want to risk them coming back."

"I should have played dead," Ember said thinking out loud. "That would have saved me a lot of pain."

"That would not have worked.," Cadell said. "Since they know nothing about me or my species, I could play dead and they wouldn't know I was faking it. You, however, those men are trained to know whether you were faking it or not."

"Yeah, I guess so," Ember sighed, pulling the bag off her shoulder. "What did he pack in here?" She muttered to herself.

She saw a blanket, a flashlight, bottles of water, granola bars, and a first aid kit.

"Bless him," Ember said. "We owe our lives to him, Cadell."

Cadell tipped his head down to the girl. "If he is still alive, then yes. Yes, we would."

"Why couldn't we have saved him? How many more butterflies have to die until they learn?" Ember shouted angrily.

Cadell bent down so that Ember could climb on. "Come on, kid. Let's leave this all behind."

"How do you know where to go? Where are we?" Ember asked, angry she didn't question Chase where they were being held captive.

"I heard the soldiers say that we were somewhere in someplace called Ohio." Cadell stated.

"Wonderful. We're in a state full of corn and a bipolar ecosystem," Ember spat bitterly.

"I don't know your geological locations like you do, but I rather feel how far the Island is away based on the queen's location." Cadell stated. "Just like how birds seem to know to fly south."

"Huh," Ember said as she climbed on her friend.

Cadell looked back and positioned himself to take off.

"Ready?" he asked.

"Yup," she replied.

With a large leap, Cadell lifted up into the air and flew from the clearing.

21

Ember could tell that Cadell was eager to get to the island as he was flying at incredible speeds. They landed a few times to let Ember relieve herself and to rest. Cadell stopped at the first water source that wasn't frozen and drank until Ember thought he was going to pop. It turned out dragons could go a long time without water, but it was uncomfortable.

Cadell landed in a warmer climate and Ember could smell the salt. It was night and the moon was shining bright in the sky. Cadell had been lucky to avoid planes by staying in the clouds. When she climbed off of her friend, she realized she was on a beach. Her mind was foggy and hazy with exhaustion.

"Quickly get done what you need to. This will be our last stop before the island. It is a long fly, but I will do my best to make it quick," said Cadell nudging Ember with his nose.

Ember nodded and did her business, before returning and stretching. She found Cadell looking out onto the ocean, the moon reflecting over the water. His markings were glowing gently and he turned his head at the approach of his partner.

"Beautiful, isn't it?" asked Ember.

"Yeah, it is," Cadell said standing to his feet and bending down.

"Why do you like sunsets, Cadell?" Ember asked.

Cadell stiffened at the sudden question and he growled. "I don't like them!"

"Oh, come on Cadell, I have seen you watching them tons of times."

Ember climbed on and Cadell waited until she was situated before taking off. She found that Cadell was right about the length of the trip. Ember began to grow bored with just water going below her. It was uninteresting unlike the trees and clouds that were beneath her before. She wondered back to the first time she had flown on the back of the dragons. Dalka had taken off without warning and she remembered being so nervous after to fly again. But now she wasn't as scared anymore.

What had changed? Ember thought as she looked at the stars above. *Maybe the fact that this creature has been through this whole journey with me and has kept me alive. I don't think that he would let me fall.*

Ember reached down and placed her hand on Cadell's shoulder. It was surprisingly quiet; the only sound was of Cadells's wings flapping. Most of the time when they flew it was windy, but the air was still and calm.

"Thank you, Cadell," Ember said.

"For?" the dragon asked, confused.

"For everything. For caring for me, for protecting me."

"Don't thank me. I told you that I am here to be whatever you need me to be. I always will be. I never thought that a human would have me wrapped around their finger, yet here I am. I am playing taxi for a female human hatchling."

Cadell laughed from beneath her. "Oddly enough, I am not repulsed or ashamed. To be honest, I am proud and really happy. I have never felt happiness like this in hundreds of years."

Ember's heart hurt for her friend. "Well, I will do my best to make it the best 80 or so years that you will ever have."

Ember could feel Cadell's shaky sigh beneath her and his flight pattern seemed to go off balance for a second.

"I...I don't want to talk about that," Cadell called back to her, his voice different than what she had ever heard. He sounded...scared.

"Are you okay, Cadell?" Ember asked, worried. That was so out of character for him.

"Yeah, I just don't want to think about the thing I have been destined to protect dying," he snapped back. "You put me through enough as it is already. I don't want everything to be thrown away in just a measly 80 years."

Ember understood that he didn't want to show her he feared losing her. It wasn't an emotion that he was used to having or comfortable showing. Her partner was stripped from his position as king, he killed people, and he wasn't ever shown love. Cadell was really something. Even after everything that he did, Ember could never bring herself to hate the dragon.

"Cadell, I could die at any time. That is just how life is. We never know when it is going to happen, but it is going to happen. That is why we must make every moment count. I would think that you would know that better than anyone," Ember pointed out. "I really feel it because look what happened to Dalka. We both left her angry, and we don't even know if we can say we are sorry."

Cadell's head lowered. "I know. I miss her too, kid. I will never forgive myself for that. But the thing with you and Dalka is that you were really the only beings that genuinely cared for me. In return, you both were really the only things I cared for. The possibility of losing Dalka...that has been the hardest thing that I have ever gone through. But it will only be second to losing you."

"I know," said Ember. "I know it is selfish, but there is only a small chance that I will have to go through the pain of losing you, so I think that I am pretty lucky."

Cadell growled and it rippled through Ember's body. "Yeah, that is selfish."

"I don't think I could really handle losing you," Ember almost whispered. "Not after I have lost so much."

"And even after all of that, you still stand. After you have been through more than the average human will ever go through in their life, you still fight. If you can handle everything up to this point, you can handle my death," Cadell gently said. "You are my partner; you are strong."

Ember smiled. "Guess I have to be to put up with you."

"What does that mean?" Cadell shouted back playfully.

Ember just laughed and Cadell shot forward, flying faster as the girl gripped on tightly. She loved the sound of the wind rushing past her ears and the fact that she felt like she could do anything on the back of Cadell. Cadell flapped his wings faster, shooting them forward. Everything melted away for a moment. All she felt was the wind, all she saw was the star-speckled sky above her, and all she smelled was the sea. She didn't remember the deaths of her friends, or the experience she had gone through at the PFIB base.

She didn't reminisce on her friends or her family, or worry about what was to become of her.

At that moment, everything was fine.

The pair soon slowed down and continued the flight in a peaceful silence. Ember began to grow tired, but she forced herself to stay awake. Cadell began to descend after what seemed to be a handful of hours and Ember saw a large island out below her.

"Is this it?" Ember asked as they neared the land.

"Yes," Cadell said. "I have to warn them of my approach. I don't want them to shoot me down. I would hold your ears."

Ember covered her ears as she could feel Cadell inhale, his sides expanded beneath her legs before he roared. The roar reverberated her body and she could still hear it clearly although she had her ears covered.

"There," he said. "Now they know it is me."

Cadell angled his wings so that he slowed his decent considerably and soared close to the trees before landing in a grassy meadow. Cadell did not lower himself so Ember could get off, but rather stayed upright. She could feel his tense muscles and his head was held high. Small puffs of smoke came from his nostrils.

Why does he seem so nervous? Ember thought. *What could possibly be scaring him?*

"If I tell you to run, you are to run. Is that understood?" Cadell said in a 'do not question me' tone.

"What?" Ember asked, scared of where he was going.

"You are to run, no matter what happens to me," Cadell said, his head turning so he could look at Ember. "Understood?"

Ember knew that she was not going to have any chance of winning any argument with the dragon. She sighed and nodded her head.

"Alright."

Cadell whirled his head around as dragons began to pour into the field. Some flew in from above while others lumbered out from the forest. She had to guess there were around twenty or so. They all had similar builds, but were different colors and sizes. The one that stood out was the pure white one with a crown.

Amrendra, thought Ember.

She suddenly heard many voices arise from the group of dragons.

"Kill the human!" she heard one yell bitterly.

"Let us kill her like they have our brethren!"

"Enough," called the white dragon. "Is this how we are going to treat the human that can save us? I asked Cadell to bring her here, she is a friend."

"How do we know?"

"Fraud! Fraud!"

"Trickery!"

"This is not the clan of dragons I lead!" the white dragon snarled, scales reflecting the high moon as her head snaked angrily. "You will obey me! I am your leader!"

The dragons quieted down as Amrendra walked through the crowd towards Ember and Cadell. The black dragon lowered his head and bowed to his leader, causing Ember to be tossed forward roughly.

"I am happy to see that you have arrived back in one piece. Is the human girl alright?" Amrendra said cocking her head slightly.

Cadell lifted his head to talk to his leader. "Yes. She will help us."

"You must be weary of the human," said a voice from behind Amrendra.

Ember peered around the leader and saw a deep purple dragon approaching. His eyes shone a bright green in the dull clearing and he cast a glance at his leader.

"No human is ever to be trusted."

"Your warning is noted, but ignored," Amrendra said. "If Cadell claims the human is helpful, then it must be so. He is a loyal dragon; his words will prove truth."

A deep growl arose from the purple dragon. Ember didn't like him, and she could tell Cadell didn't either from the growl that he tossed back.

"Your concern is not needed, Jassco. Make yourself useful and tend to the wounds of our friend," Amrendra said sternly to the bristling dragon.

Jassco nodded and lumbered off after throwing a glare at the two newcomers.

"Return to your nest," Amrendra called out. "There is no need for concern, I will handle the situation from here."

The dragons in the clearing broke apart, some staying and mumbling among themselves while others departed back the way they had come. Ember watched the scene unfold with wide eyes. She hadn't realized that she had been gripping onto one of Cadell's spikes as tightly as she had and let go.

"There is no need for fear, young one," said Amrendra, coming up to the pair.

Cadell lowered himself and allowed Ember to get off. She looked up at the white dragon and she was awestruck on how beautiful she was.

Her scales were a pure white, there was no other color on her scales. Her eyes also shown a deep blue, exactly like Cadell's.

Cadell was not kidding, Ember thought as she studied the dragons before her. *They really were born to look like leaders.*

"Come, you both must be exhausted. Let us get you something to eat and quench your thirst," the white dragon said as she turned.

Ember followed behind and Cadell followed suit. Amrendra lead them up a steep mountain that wound up to a cliff. The path was wide and had been worn down. Before they reached the top, a cave opened on the side of the mountain where the leader led them. When Ember stepped inside, she saw that it was lit up by a large crystal in the center of the ceiling. It was a large room that smelled of herbs. She saw dragons laying on beds of leaves and saw many different types of berries and plants on large rocks that acted as tables.

It's like a hospital, Ember realized as she looked around. Suddenly, Ember's eyes landed on a familiar frame.

"Dalka?" Ember asked.

"Little one?" said the dragon as she lifted her head.

Ember could see that she was injured, wrapped in vines and leaves, they acted like bandages. They shifted as the dragon heaved herself to stand, her eyes happy as she approached the two.

"Dalka!" Cadell exclaimed happily.

Ember watched as the normally cool and collected dragon ran over to Dalka and nuzzled underneath her chin. His tail that waved loosely in the air showed his pleasure and happiness.

"How are you alive? We thought that we lost you!" Cadell cried as he sat next to her.

Ember could tell that the turquoise dragon was weak, but the strength that shown in her eyes was never stronger.

"Jassco saved me," Dalka said.

"What was he doing so far from the island?" Cadell asked.

"I asked the same thing. He said that he had come looking for us. I can't even tell you how lucky I was when he found me. He had just a little Merocomee left to save me. I was basically dead when he came," Dalka explained.

Ember walked up to the dragon, tears brimming in her eyes as Dalka bent her head down to Ember. The girl hugged the dragon's head as she cried, overwhelmed with emotion from seeing her friend she thought she had lost.

"I missed you," Ember sniffed.

"And I, you," Dalka murmured.

"If we are done with your gathering, I would like to put this human's power to work as soon as possible," a voice said from the entrance of the cave. Ember looked and saw Jassco peering in, purple scales reflecting the moon.

"Why don't we talk to the Elders first?" Dalka suggested. "They will know about the powers and can help us so we can use them to their full extent."

Jassco nodded. "Good idea, Dalka. I will call them over since you are still injured."

The dragon disappeared and the three were left alone again.

"Is Jack..." Dalka asked looking at both Ember and Cadell.

"Yes," Ember said. "He died in my arms before you came. Drake and Jane were already dead."

"That is such a shame," Dalka said closing her eyes. "I will miss them all."

The two dragons and Ember turned their heads as a group of seven dragons entered the room where they were gathered. They were all dull colors and Ember could tell they were older. More than half the dragons had wings, while the rest did not and were smaller and lighter than the rest. Ember had to guess that they were the Elders Dalka had spoken about.

Ember saw Cadell and Dalka bow and Ember followed suit not wanting to disrespect or be out of place. When Ember looked up, she saw the Elders bowing to them. Dalka and Cadell's face showed they were in shock, making Ember believe that this did not happen very often.

"I am honored," Dalka stammered.

"As am I," Cadell added.

"You deserved it," said a light blue dragon, sounding female. "You almost got yourself killed, all of you did, and you completed the mission you set out to do. We are all very proud of you."

Dalka and Cadell did not say anything, clearly too shocked. A dark golden dragon stepped forward and began to speak.

"I will tell you what we know from the prophecy. As you can see, there are no longer twelve of us. We lost five since you've been gone." The golden dragon sounded male. He paused to allow the news of the passing to sink in before he continued. "I know about energy transfer. Cadell, you can give energy to your partner, and your partner can give energy to you. You do not have to be in contact, but you do have to be within eyesight. This transfer can only be done between you and your partner."

"We have already figured that out," Cadell said. Ember could tell he was trying to keep his cool. "We know how to create Merocomee stones, and how to heal dragons too. I also know how to make my markings glow."

"What about the water?" A pale orange dragon called.

"We know about that too," seethed Cadell.

"To be honest, that is all we know as well." the golden dragon said as he stepped back. If Ember didn't know better, he almost seemed embarrassed.

"You are kidding," Cadell said between gritted teeth.

"Well, I do know what the markings do," said a green dragon. "It is a show of your power. Often times it will make attackers a bit weary of you."

"A damn bird could have told me that!" Cadell snapped.

"That is all we have to offer you," said the blue dragon who had first spoken.

Ember could see Cadell was royally pissed at the lack of information that they had been given. Ember walked over and placed her hand on the dragon's tense shoulder in an effort to calm him.

"Thank you," said Dalka as she bowed once more, trying her best to get rid of the Elders before Cadell exploded on them.

Ember and Cadell tersely bowed and watched them retreat.

"Well, that was a waste of time," Cadell spat. "And we thought of them as all high and mighty. We figured this all out on our own."

Dalka sighed but did not protest the statement. She seemed to agree. "Maybe it was just our luck that the other five died. They must have had the missing information."

"I am sorry you are disappointed. But look at the bright side!" Ember said. "At least we don't have to spend any time learning anything new!"

"That we know of..." muttered Cadell.

"So, what is up with the Elders?" Ember asked. "What makes them so 'high and mighty'?"

"Originally, there were twelve clans of dragons. Each clan had a dragon that was the oldest who held sacred information. The second oldest became the Elder in training. The Elder would pass on all the information to the Elder in training before they passed. After the Elder passed, the Elder in training would become the new Elder and another Elder in training would be appointed.

"The Elders of all the clans rarely ever got together all at once, and it was only in times of peril. It happened for the first time when the plague started. That is how the prophecy came about. All of the twelve dragons had a piece of the prophecy and they were able to piece it together.

"Before we left, they told us some of the information, but they would not reveal all of it. They are forbidden to tell some information at given times."

Dalka cast a look around her before she continued.

"To be honest, they should have just told us everything they knew. Then, when the other Elders died, we wouldn't be missing information."

Ember nodded in understanding. She turned her head suddenly when she heard steps approaching. Both dragons and the girl turned their heads to see Jassco appear.

"May I take the human?" He asked, clearly unsure of how to approach the situation.

Ember glanced back at her two friends and Dalka flashed the girl an encouraging smile.

"Go on Ember! This is it!" Dalka encouraged.

Ember took a breath and walked to Jassco and she heard Cadell following behind her.

"Cadell, I would prefer if you did not come along," the purple dragon growled.

"Excuse me?" Cadell snarled, tail lashing as he took a step forward.

"Cadell," Dalka said gently. "Let him do this. Let us finally be saved."

Cadell sighed and backed down as Jassco flashed Dalka a smile.

"Thank you, dear," Jassco said sweetly. "Come, human," he said ushering Ember to follow him.

"I have a name, you know!" Ember snapped as she followed the beast.

The dragon rolled his eyes and flicked his tail. "I won't be disrespected by your kind," Jassco spat.

"Then I won't help you," Ember said crossing her arms and refusing to follow.

Jassco stopped and snarled, whirling around to face Ember.

"You know, I was going to go further away so no one could hear us, but I think I can get the deed done fast enough before anyone notices," Jassco snapped as he roughly grabbed Ember and threw her against the side of a wall.

"Now, first I want you to make twenty Merocomee stones. If you don't comply, I will kill you." Jassco dropped the girl and Ember immediately began to make the stones, not liking how the dragon stared at her. She made the desired amount and then turned to leave, but Jassco grabbed her again and she let out a scream.

"Shut up! If you do anything to go against me, I will kill your family. I know exactly where they are. I will not hesitate to kill them," Jassco snarled.

Ember, knowing that Cadell had heard her scream and was coming, spat in the dragon's face. "Rot in hell!" she screamed.

"Oh, trust me. Since I let this plague loose on the island and in the states, I have no doubt that's where I am going," Jassco sneered.

He dropped the girl as Cadell lunged at him as the purple dragon took off into the night sky. He roared after Jassco and snarled, snaking his head as the dragon got away. Ember could tell Cadell was still exhausted from the escape from the PFIB base as he did not chase the other dragon.

"What did he do?" he snarled.

"Made me make all of those," she said gesturing to all the Merocomee stones that laid around her. "But he told me he is the one who set the plague loose. He said that he was going to kill my family. I can't let that happen, Cadell," Ember said frantically.

"It won't. I will have someone synthesize this Merocomme in order to heal me and Dalka. We will set off soon," Cadell said.

Ember watched as he called dragons and ordered them. She saw Amrendra come from the cave after the commotion and watched as the two talked. Cadell looked like he fit with the queen, and it made Ember's heart hurt that it wasn't meant to be. A red dragon came forward to the Merocomee stones.

"This is the healer from another clan," Cadell said as he came over to Ember. "Since Jassco was our original healer, he was automatically going to be the one to do this. However, since he is gone, she will do the same thing." Cadell stopped for a moment and looked in the direction that Jassco had taken off. "This doesn't make any sense. We need to get answers."

Ember watched as the red dragon took a stone that had been carved into a bowl and place the Merocomee inside. The Dragon took her claw and drew a shape on the stone and then blew a light blue flame over it. When the fire ceased, Ember saw a light pink metallic liquid in place of the stone.

"Quick! Take a sip," the red dragon said giving the bowl to Cadell.

Cadell dipped his muzzle and his markings flashed. Ember could almost feel the power coming off the dragon as his health was restored. Cadell then gave the bowl to Dalka who had walked in right after Amrendra. She too sipped the healing liquid and was healed instantly.

Ember climbed onto the back of Cadell who had bent down and was awaiting Ember. But before both dragons and the girl could take off, she heard Amrendra call for them from behind.

"Wait! I am coming with you!"

Ember almost fell off when Cadell turned quickly to face his queen. "You can't! It is too dangerous!" Cadell snapped.

Amrendra did not seem to hear and the white dragon bent her head to drink the Merocomee. She ran forward and leapt into the sky, and Ember understood that it was their signal to follow.

Cadell pushed off from the ledge and flapped his wings in order to keep up with Amrendra. Dalka followed in pursuit and the three dragons began their trip back to which it started; Maytown, Montana.

22

Cadell landed after a few hours of flying. The sun was beginning to rise and Ember knew that they only had a little time to make it back to her family before Jassco. Ember slid off Cadell, body aching and sore from the long flight. She was exhausted from lack of sleep and it made her body feel like lead. Although she had managed to rest for a bit on the dragon, it was not enough to let her body heal. Ember was the most uncomfortable she had ever been, from the oily hair and grimy clothes, she felt utterly disgusting. She shook it off, knowing now wasn't the time to complain. She stretched and yawned, looking at the three dragons who stood around her.

"Why don't you hunt?" Ember asked. "There is a good chance that the deer around here are not infected."

"We could," Dalka said thoughtfully. "But we can't leave you here alone right now, and we need to reach your family."

Ember smiled, thankful that the dragon was keeping her in mind. Cadell walked over to her and bent down, allowing her to get on his back. Amrendra, who had remained quiet the whole flight finally spoke.

"Do any of you mind if I stay back to eat?" Amrendra asked quietly.

Ember could tell the dragon was embarrassed. But Ember could see that compared to Dalka and Cadell, she was much thinner.

"No, not at all," Ember said.

"But how will you be able to find us?" Dalka asked. "We can sense you, but you can't us. If only Cadell was a king,"

"I am not king," Cadell snarled bitterly.

"You're not king *yet*," Amrendra corrected.

The white dragon walked over to Cadell and looked him in the eyes. Ember watched as Cadell returned the stare with even intensity.

"You would have not been born a leader unless you were destined to become one. Just because you didn't become king right away does not mean you will never be. Sometimes, time is needed to allow you to grow." Amrendra began. "Thus, I believe that you are ready. I have been watching you ever since you came. You have changed completely, Cadell. A king and queen are not meant to be perfect, but they are meant to be the best they can. You have become wiser, stronger, and most importantly, you learned about compassion. We must be humble and kind as leaders."

Amrendra stopped for a moment and she glanced at Ember.

"If I am not wrong Cadell, this human girl has to be a huge part in the change you went through. I know that you are ready. I am ready to finally have someone to help me rule and become my mate. I am ready to accept you as king, but it depends on if you are ready to accept being king."

Ember watched as Cadell dropped his gaze, clearly at a loss for what to say or how to act. When the dragon seemed to have prepared what he wanted to say, he looked at his queen and he offered her a rare, genuine smile.

"You are correct. Ember is the main thing that got me to change. If it wasn't for her, I would have never learned from the mistakes I made in the past. I owe her." He paused, casting a glance behind him to Ember, who sat on his back. He then turned to Dalka and he bowed. "But who I also owe just as much to is Dalka. Yes, we may have gotten at each other's throats, but she kept me sane through the whole trip. I do not know what I would have done without her. When I thought I had lost her, I have never had something affect me as deeply as that."

Ember looked over and she saw Dalka looking at Cadell with the most touched look that she had ever seen. Ember knew that what Cadell had said meant everything to Dalka.

Cadell stood and looked at the white dragon. "Yes, I am ready to accept being king."

Cadell lowered himself so that Ember could get off. She slid off and went over to Dalka who stood watching them with a very proud look on her face. She watched as Amrendra bowed to Cadell and he roared, shooting fire into the air as his marking's glowed. When the fire died down, Ember saw that Cadell seemed different. He was confident and proud, his head held high and with power.

Ember saw Cadell reach over and nuzzle Amrendra gently, and she saw that the white dragon returned the affection to him. For the first time, Ember saw Cadell truly happy.

Amrendra laughed and looked around. "I think it might be best to stay with you. I can hunt later; I will be alright. I can hold out a bit longer I suppose.

Cadell briskly walked over to Ember and bent down, allowing her on his back once more. When she settled, he jumped into the air and continued the flight back to her hometown.

The group stayed high above the clouds and flew fast. Ember's stomach churned in anxiety as she worried about her mother and father. She may not be happy with them, she may never return to live with them again, but she would be damned if she ever stopped loving them.

They were her family, and nothing was going to take that away from her.

Ember lost track of time as they continued to fly, and spent her time watching the clouds below her. When Cadell suddenly slowed, Ember looked at the dragon with a questioning look.

As if sensing the girl's suspicion, Cadell explained himself. "We are here, but we don't know what course of action we want to take."

"What do you mean you don't know what course of action you want to take?" Ember snapped. "Let's go down there and save my family."

"It's not that simple, Ember," Dalka said from Cadell's side. "If we go down there in broad daylight, PFIB will know of our location and be on us like bloodhounds."

"PFIB works above the law," Ember said. "What they are doing is illegal. I am home now; your dragons and the illness are being healed back on the island. We have nothing to lose, we can expose PFIB to the government and have them shut down like Jack said."

"But won't they just capture us?" Amrendra said. "The government won't let us go or help us!"

"Not if we make it known to the public what happened," Ember smiled as she formulated a plan. "And I know just the person who will help us. But first I need to save my family."

Cadell seeing the panic Ember was in immediately began his descent. At first, the clouds were too thick to see anything, but once the group got past the blanket of clouds, the scene unfolded in front of her, much to Ember's horror.

Her home, the one that she had grown up in was burning. Everything was completely destroyed.

Ember knew that it was not PFIB, as everything was destroyed recently, and Jassco was standing in the middle of the wreckage with her parents beneath his talons. He looked like a mischievous cat proud of his destruction.

"I told you!" Jassco howled up into the sky as he saw the group approaching. "I warned you of what I would do!"

"Jassco! What are you doing? Stop this!" Amrendra called as she landed.

Cadell stayed up in the air, and Ember knew he wasn't going to land in fear of getting Ember in danger. Dalka landed next to Amrendra and faced the dragon.

"Let them go," the turquoise dragon snarled.

"No! They must die!" he spat.

"Why are you doing this?" Amrendra asked, clearly trying her best to keep the composure together.

"The girl is ruining our plan! I need to make her suffer, and then we can bend her to our will. She is useless if she believes that she is independent."

"She has as much right to freedom as we do!" Amrendra snapped. "She is willing to help us! Stop!"

"No. I told you she is ruining the PFIB plan," Jassco sneered.

"Why the hell are you affiliated with PFIB?" Dalka snarled. "He killed my son! Don't you remember? Don't you care for the pain that I was put through? I thought you were my ally, Jassco. I have known you for centuries! What has happened to you?"

The purple dragon just shrugged and seemed bored with the conversation.

"They promised to save my life. They were going to release the plague onto the island. PFIB found the island location and it was only a matter of time before they figured out a way to get onto it without us noticing. But they offered to spare me and my mate if I set it loose for them. I will not and am not going to die and neither is she."

"They are brainwashing you!" Dalka said. "They are just going to kill you after this is over!"

"It is doubtful," Jassco snapped. "I am one of the best assets that they ever had."

"I cannot be angry at you for wanting to live," Amrendra said. "But you could have told us instead of releasing it onto the island without our knowing! We could have avoided this whole thing!"

"They took Atlas," Jassco said. "I didn't want her to die, and I didn't want to die. They told me once this is all over, they would reunite us."

Atlas, Ember thought. The name sounded familiar. At first, she didn't remember, and then it hit her. *Atlas was the dragon that got killed at the PFIB base. That was the dragon*

Chase was talking about.

"She is dead," Ember called out. "They lied to you. They killed her. A soldier told me about it when we were captured."

"No, you are the liar!" Jassco said lunging into the air, dropping her limp parents on the ground.

Ember saw the purple dragon fast approaching Cadell and felt her stomach drop as the dragon made a rapid descent to the ground. Ember felt herself fly off the back of the dragon and land harshly onto the ground. She looked up and saw Cadell lunge at Jassco as he tried to reach her. Her partner attacked the purple dragon, biting his wing and clawing his chest. Ember watched as Amrendra and Dalka too joined in to help take down the dragon. She heard Jassco snarling and growling as he fought. Ember knew that he did not want to be taken down, the uncertainty of what was going to happen once they did get him pinned, fueled him. They were able to pin him to the ground and all three dragons stood on top of him, snarling.

"It is over," Amrendra said. "Give it up!"

"On the contrary," said a voice behind Ember.

She felt a warm arm wrap around her body and she felt a cold barrel pressed against the side of her head. Ember knew that Penser was pressing a gun to her head, but she did not know what the man wanted.

"Let the dragon go or I'll kill the girl," Penser said.

She watched as the three dragons let Jassco go and he flew up into the air out of reach. Ember saw the three dragons looking at her worried.

"We let him go, now let the girl go," Cadell snarled.

"Ah ah ah, not so fast," Penser sneered. "You first need

to tell us how to get on the island."

"No!" Amrendra snarled. "Just let her go!"

Ember heard Penser cock the pistol. "Three seconds until I kill her just like I killed that hatchling of yours, lizard." The last statement was directed at Dalka and Ember knew it.

He killed Zimmeran, Ember realized.

She saw Dalka's face scrunch up in rage and she knew she only had seconds to act. She took her leg and lifted it up as hard as she could backwards, right in between Penser's legs. She leapt out of the way as soon as his grip faltered and she heard the pistol go off behind her. She ducked just as Dalka came lunging at Penser. She scrambled up and ran just in time to see dozens of soldiers burst out from the trees. Ember ducked under a tree and watched as both Amrendra and the new king shot flames from their mouths, burning everything around them

She heard a roar from above and watched as Jassco flew from the sky and rammed into Dalka, sending her flying onto the ground. Dalka got up and roared, angered that she had been attacked. Ember looked behind the dragon to see that Penser was dead.

"Why are you stopping me?" growled Dalka.

"Because! I am not about to be killed because of your need for revenge!" Jassco snarled.

"He killed my son!" Dalka howled running at him. She took a hold of his wing and she heard an audible crack as the wing broke. She heard Jassco roar in pain and he whirled around, biting Dalka's muzzle.

Jassco looked around him and saw Ember. They locked eyes for a moment, burning hatred mixed with a fearful haze was the only thing that both creatures saw in each other's eyes. The purple dragon pushed off his friend and lunged at Ember. His jaws open in a menacing snarl, Ember watched as he came closer and she braced for impact. When it never came, she saw a bulk of turquoise in front of her and realized it was Dalka.

Ember did not know how she managed to beat the dragon, but Ember did not question.

"I have lost one of my hatchlings and I will be damned if I lose another." Dalka snarled.

"You really think of that, that, wretched *human* as your own kin?" Jassco snapped disgusted. "I am ashamed to call you a dragon."

Ember watched as Amrendra was fending off soldiers with her tail and talons and Cadell was shooting fire at whoever got close. Ember could feel the hot flames and it burned her skin. Her attention was turned back to the dragon in front of her as she lunged at Jassco. She heard Dalka roar as Jassco was able to pin her beneath him.

"Dalka!" Ember yelled.

Before anyone could move, Jassco bit down on Dalka's neck. Cadell, seeing what was happening, flew over top of Ember and grabbed the dragon from the back of his neck with his strong jaws. He slammed him into a tree, his markings pulsating with fury.

"You. Are. Dead." Cadell stated, and he then lunged at Jassco's neck, before biting down on his windpipe, killing him instantly.

Ember scrambled over to Dalka who was moaning and trying her best to stand, but she saw the dragon losing too much blood. When she saw Ember approaching, she stopped and bent her head over to the girl. Ember immediately put her hands on the dragon, trying her best to heal and give her energy, but she wasn't able to heal faster than Dalka was dying.

"My little one," Dalka said turning her head to put her muzzle in Ember's chest. "You are the strongest being I have ever known. You were such a brave woman. I am proud of you, my love."

Ember watched as Cadell approached and bent his head to the dying dragon.

"No, Dalka," Cadell said closing his eyes. "Please don't go."

"Oh, Cadell," Dalka sighed. "You were my child too, just like Ember. Not by blood, but by heart. I am so proud of you, my son."

"Dalka, don't!" Ember screamed.

"It's okay, little one," Dalka soothed.

Ember could see Dalka was growing weaker.

"I am ready to see...my son." Dalka sighed resting her head on the ground.

Ember saw Dalka's eyes close and watched as her sides stopped breathing. She held onto Dalka's neck and sobbed, fully feeling the pain of the loss.

Dalka was dead.

23

It took Ember and Cadell a moment to gain their composure. They both knew that she was gone, but neither wanted to believe it. When Ember had no more tears left to cry, she walked over to her parents who were laying where Jassco had dropped them. She bent down to check their pulse and found them still alive. Ember knew what she needed to do from there.

"Cadell, I need you to fly me somewhere. We are going to finish this." Cadell lowered himself and allowed Ember to get on his back. "Amrendra? Can you stay here with my parents and make sure they are safe? I will return."

Amrendra nodded.

Cadell took off and allowed Ember to guide him. "Fly low. I want as many people to see you as possible."

"What?" Cadell snapped bitterly. "This is suicide!"

"No, trust me," Ember said.

She instructed Cadell to land in front of a house and he did so. Cars swerved and she saw police cars fast approaching. She ran up to the door and pounded.

"Taylor! It is me, Ember!" Ember yelled.

Before she could even knock again, the door whirled

open and Taylor tackled Ember in an embrace.

"Ember I thought I lost you! I am so sorry for everything I—"

"There is no time to explain. Is your mother home? I need her to get me on the news now," Ember interrupted.

Taylor saw the dragon behind Ember and the police cars. "What the hell did you get yourself into, Ember?" Taylor asked.

"Please! Come with me and I will explain, but I need your help! There is no way I can do this without you!"

Taylor looked in Ember's eyes and smiled. "Let's go."

Ember grabbed her friend's hand and helped her on the back of Cadell. She could tell her friend was nervous, but Ember did her best to keep her calm.

Cadell took off and she heard Taylor scream. Cadell's wings bumped Taylor's legs since they were not up high enough, but he managed to make it work. He went high into the clouds and lost the police cars below them, before landing in the clearing where Ember had first met the dragons.

Ember got off of Cadell, looking around and noticing how it had changed since she had been there last. The tracks the dragons had made were still there, and Ember ran her hand over a smaller one that was near her feet, knowing Dalka had left them.

"What is going on?" Taylor asked confused.

"This is Cadell," Ember said motioning to the black dragon behind her. "I was a part of the prophecy to save their island from a plague started by an agency called PFIB. They work above the law and basically everything they are doing is illegal. I need to expose them before the rest of the group gets on the island to kill the rest of the dragons that are left. They just killed one of our best dragon friends, and I need help. The only way we can do this is if we tell the people what has happened and make sure they are on our side. If we immediately go to the government, they will be liable to just take the dragons and study them. If we get the general public on our side, there will be outcry and the government will not risk that. Can you get your mother here with a camera?"

Taylor smiled and flipped open her phone. "I am on it."

* * * * *

By the time Taylor's mother had arrived, both the police and PFIB officials had arrived due to the news outlets request for police and FBI backup. Ember, Taylor, and Cadell were questioned and they revealed everything that had happened over the course of the last couple weeks. After hearing everything that had happened with PFIB, calls began to be made and all PFIB officials on sight began to be immediately arrested.

The FBI at first denied Ember and Cadell to be shown on TV, but with a fierce growl from Cadell, they soon obliged. Before Ember and Cadell were set to go on, Ember heard someone fighting the police officers.

"Hey! Let me go! I know her! I am not with them!" A voice cried.

"Oh yeah. Sure, you're not. You're wearing the damn uniform!" an officer spat.

Ember looked over to see Chase being handcuffed. She sprinted over to the officer and started to yell.

"Wait! Wait! He is right, he helped me!" Ember said.

The officer let him go and Ember ran over to Chase, tackling him in an embrace.

"I thought you died!" Ember said.

"I thought you died!" Chase laughed. "When I heard of a girl and a dragon, I hightailed it over here to find you."

"Do you think you could help us? With this whole TV thing? I mean you were part of PFIB, you have to know all the corruption behind it," Ember asked, looking up at Chase hopeful.

Chase looked over at the FBI officers. "Do I get witness protection if I do this?"

"We can make arrangements," one officer said hanging his thumbs off his belt.

"Then I will do it," Chase agreed.

They both walked over to where Cadell was and the large dragon dropped his head down to the young soldier.

"Boy, I thank you for saving our lives. I am in debt to you," Cadell said quietly.

"That is the nicest thing you are going to get from him," Ember laughed. "I would take it and treasure that."

"Are you ready?" Taylor called over from where she was helping her mother and a camera crew.

It was in that moment Ember had no idea what she was going to say. She had been more worried about getting the things together that she had not planned what she was going to say.

"What am I going to say?" Ember asked, looking at Chase in fear.

"Just say what you think you have to say," Chase said. "If the prophecy says you're going to save the dragons, then I have no doubt you're going to do just that. Let this come from your heart. Tell the struggles that you faced, and tell the truth."

Ember nodded and she took the microphone that was handed to her. Chase also received one and a reporter stepped in front of a camera, clearly eager to get her part of the spotlight.

"3,2,1, and live!" a crewman shouted.

"We are live here in Maytown, Montana with a teen girl that has been missing for over a month. She is here to tell her remarkable story in hopes that she can shed some light on the events that have led to the recent headlines on dragons."

The reporter stepped back and Ember knew that this was it. What she said, could either make or break what happened after. This was going to go down in history. She adjusted the microphone in her sweaty hands before taking a deep breath and beginning.

"Hello, I am Ember Winters, this is my partner, Cadell, and this is my friend, Chase. I owe my lives to both of these two."

Ember looked straight into the camera, and with the help of Chase, she relayed the story and all the details she could remember.

Ember stopped for a moment and reached up to touch Cadell's nose. "We are not so different. All they want is to rebuild their life and live in harmony alongside humans, but they cannot do that unless the government offers them protection and promises not to attack them. I can say, after meeting the dragons, they are more compassionate than most of humanity, and if they are going to do anything, they are only going to make the world better. But in order for that to happen, we need everyone to help. We need petitions, we need protests, and we need change. We need to show the government that this is not just what we want, not just what the dragons want, but what all of us need."

Ember took Chase's hand and Cadell bent his head near Ember. "Because if we all work together and have faith, then there is nothing in this world that we can't do."

When Ember had finished, she looked over and saw her mother and father standing with Amrendra next to the rows of military vehicles and police cars.

"Mom, Dad," Ember choked. She ran over and hugged them both. She could feel the sobs racking both of her parents' bodies as she embraced them. She felt her father move her back and she looked into his eyes. For the first time in years, she could tell that he was sober.

"Ember, I am so sorry for everything that I have done. I have no excuse and I hope that you can find it in your heart to forgive me," her father told her.

Ember, still overcome with emotion, looked at her father. She knew that just like Cadell, her father was learning. It would be hard for Ember to forget that past, but her father realized his mistake and was fixing it. She wrapped him in a hug, but did not say a word.

The FBI agents approached her parents and they began to talk to them about a new home. Ember however did not mind, as she knew that everything was over and she no longer had to worry. She felt Cadell come up behind her and nuzzle her hair.

"You did good, kid. Dalka and Jack would have been proud."

Epilogue

Ember knew that now, everything was okay. The newscast went viral and people from all around the globe pitched in to help. It all played out perfectly as if it was fate, and she felt as if the prophecy had something to do with it. The government had no other choice but to give in and help the dragons.

Ember and her family moved down to Florida, knowing it was the shortest distance for the dragons to travel in order to see Ember and her family. Ember was able to help cure the dragons and rid the Island once and for all from the deadly plague. Ember also helped discover a way to reverse the plague in the United States.

Ember became close friends with Chase, and the two worked closely together in order to fulfill a project they both created; they both wanted to rebuild PFIB. Both Chase and Ember wanted PFIB to become an organization that educated people about the dragons and promoted alliances with them. It was a very hard start at first, but Chase was able to get it started. Within a matter of months, both Chase and Ember were the head of a massive life-changing organization.

Cadell and Amrendra began to rebuild the Island back to its former glory. Ember visited often and saw that they created statues in honor of Drake, Jane, Jack and Dalka. Ember visited the statues every time she came in order to remember her lost friends.

Cadell and Ember grew closer every day, and Ember knew that the rest of her life would be spent with the dragons.

Ember stood watching the group of dragons who remained on the island perform a ritual that had been practiced for ages. She watched as Cadell stood in the middle of the circles, as the remaining elders gave him their blessings. He bowed his head and the blue elder stepped forth, revealing a golden necklace with rubies encrusted inside. The elder placed the necklace over Cadell's head and the king raised his head to look at the dragons surrounding him. All the dragons bowed, showing their respect to their new leader and Ember stood smiling in awe. As the dragons were still bowed, Cadell cast a glance over his shoulder to Ember, and flashed her a genuine smile.

"To Drake!" hollered Cadell.

"To Drake!" all the dragons repeated.

"To Jane!"

"To Jane!"

"To Jack!"

"To Jack!"

"To Dalka!"

"To Dalka!"

Cadell roared, his markings glowing brightly and flames shooting out of his mouth. All of the dragons followed suit. Ember watched them cheer and celebrate among themselves. Ember knew that she could never let it go. She would never forget those who saved her, the dragons, and molded her into the person she was meant to be.

THE END

Acknowledgements

Emily Tilton: For being my anchor and my rock through this entire journey. For setting up the meetings, writing my notes, and telling me I was good enough. You did it all. You're my superhero.

Michael Tilton: For helping me keep my promise and pushing me to be the best person I can be.

Bonnie Bryant AKA 'Mimi': For reviewing and being the first person to read my book.

Trooper: For being my drive and my rock.

Chloe Burt: For your inspirational mind, your kind spirit, and the 'we are not so different' idea.

Ryan O' Neal of Sleeping at Last: For all your music that helped me through those 4 am writing nights.

Janine Hvizdos: For creating my cover and bringing my dragons to life.

About the Author

Hi! I am the author of Ember's Dragons, and I wanted to personally thank you for taking the time to read this book.

This book came to me on a vacation trip in 2016 when I was 14 years old. It has been such an amazing journey being able to write this book and to make these characters come to life. Although the journey was a very long and hard one, it is one that I plan to do again and again in the future.

I believe that anyone can create something they are proud of. On the outside, I come across as someone who is justifiably considered normal. I have a passion for horses, reading, writing, and drawing. I have a horse who I love dearly and I will be attending college soon. These things are common, but I strive to do the uncommon.

Although I am comfortable with the simplicities that I have, my heart longs for something more. I have always known I was going to change the world. While I never really knew how or when, I knew I was going to do it through my writing. My goal is to provide a place where people can go to escape, learn, and relax. I want my books to not only entertain my readers, but to be used as a vessel, as a drive for people to create something of their own to better understand the world around them.

I firmly believe knowledge is something you can't put a price on. Knowledge is not only understanding facts, but it is having a deeper understanding of the universe and the part that you play. Through creating worlds and characters, I have gotten a deeper understanding of this. Although I will never know it all, I plan to dive deep and learn as much as I can in order to help people.

I hope that as you read this book, you learned more about yourself. My goal as a writer is that you take something away from each of my books and apply it to an important aspect of your life. I want to change life for the better. And if I can change at least one, than this book has done its purpose.